THE FIRE ON MEMORY LANE

A Novella

Felix I.D. Dimaro

THE FIRE ON MEMORY LANE

Written by FELIX I.D. DIMARO

Cover Artwork: Rosco Nischler
Interior Artwork: Zach Horvath; Rosco Nischler
Typography and Graphic Design: Courtney Swank
Editor: Alessandra Sztrimbely

ALSO BY
FELIX I.D. DIMARO

How To Make A Monster
The Loveliest Shade of Red

BUG SPRAY
A Tale of ~~Love and~~ Madness

VIRAL LIVES
A Ghost Story

2222

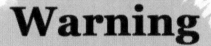

Warning

This story contains
mature content,
including explicit language,
scenes depicting sex,
and references to suicide.

Discretion is advised.

For everyone who has had to live with regret.
And for those who were unable to do so.

"If only I could turn back time."
— Everyone Everywhere Ever

1

It started with a bad day. One in a string of many.

A string that had created a bad week, a bad month, a bad year... You get the picture.

For Connor Michaels, this particular bad day was the culmination of several bad years. Connor, the ex-husband. Connor, who once upon a time had been a father of two, that number now diminished. Connor who, already in the middle of an incredibly bad day, was currently in his living room doing his best to make sure the rest of his day would be no better. Guaranteeing beyond doubt that tomorrow would be worse.

Because nothing makes a bad day worse than cleaning up after your own temper tantrum. And Connor was having a tantrum of epic proportions. It was the result of all of those bad days and weeks and years that had made up this mostly bad half-decade. A rage brought on when Connor realized that, after all of those terrible times in his life – all of which were followed by promises and lies, assurances that things would inevitably get better – this day had been waiting for him. It had been waiting to spring out and announce itself as the worst of his bad days. A 'worst' day, after the days which had made up the life he had led over the last several years, was a hard thing to fathom. Something he would have said was impossible. Not after the accident.

Not after the funeral. The tiny little urn.

Not after the divorce. Not after all of that.

He had thought the worst of his days were behind him, no matter how bad they still typically were. Today had made him realize how much of a fool he had been.

Connor had just finished flipping over his coffee table, sending it flying across his small living room, causing the table to hit the wall and lose a leg before falling to the floor. Where it hit the wall, it had left a hole between a couple of dollar store paintings that were supposed to add some measure of ambiance to this run-down one-level shack of a home. Connor looked at the hole before walking over to the wall and adding another, then another. With his fists, he added more. With his head smashing through the drywall, another hole. More...

The couch was already upside down, the side table in splinters beside it on the ground. In the kitchen – where this tantrum had started after he had poured himself a cup of tap water that had tasted slightly like cheese – a step couldn't be taken without walking over broken glass, shattered dishware, overturned and spilled cutlery, canned goods. Food of all nature.

Connor had gone straight to the kitchen when he had gotten home less than fifteen minutes prior. Had decided not to get right into the whiskey, as he usually did. Because, only an hour before his tantrum had begun, he had tried to talk to *her*, and *she* had called him a drunk. Had told him to get his life together. And then she had actually done it. She had moved across the country and taken his daughter and the remains of his son with her. And now he was left with nothing.

That's what had been on his mind when he had taken the sip of the foul-tasting water. The funky water he had decided to drink instead of the whiskey that would have made him feel slightly better about what had just happened.

2

Or at least slightly numb to it. The water had been the straw that had crippled one very overburdened camel. After sipping it, his mind had gone vacant even as it filled with nothing. The word:

Nothing.

That word took up all of his mind. Nothing.

Because it was all he had left.

All that remained of the family he had built. Nothing.

To look forward to, to dream of, to be hopeful for. Nothing.

Nothing, nothing, nothing, nothing...

"Nothing! That fucking whore left me with *nothing*!" He had screamed as he had taken that foul-tasting water and the glass cup which held it and smashed it on the dirty kitchen floor. The sound of it shattering was like music — cathartic notes to a dismal tune. And Connor had made it his goal to create a score to the rest of his day.

It was a plate next. Smashed. Another cup. Shattered. Two cups. Then three more. Mugs, bowls, plate, plate, plate, plate. All to smithereens. Pots, pans. Everything. Until the cabinets held the same nothing that he was screaming of. Until the cabinets matched his life.

He was still shouting variations of that one sentence as he marauded through his home, now in his living room, punching and headbutting holes in the wall, not realizing he was only moments away from his neighbor calling the police on him. And not for the first time.

The next time he wound up in a jail cell, he might not get out so easily. He had been in the drunk tank earlier this year for being rowdy at a bar, and the local cops had taken a disliking to him. Especially since he had already been labeled something terrible. Given a tag by this entire town he had once been so popular in. This town where he was now considered to be something far worse than the nothing he believed himself to be.

They had labeled him a child killer. More specifically, they thought he was responsible for the death of his own son. Marked a negligent dad. A nothing of a father.

He had been about to punch another hole in the wall – there were close to ten of them now. And he would have made ten more – but he noticed for the first time that the television was on. Noticed it. Then noticed that he hadn't noticed it the entire time he had been back in his home, smashing things. Didn't remember ever turning it on. Not sure why he would have. But it seemed that, all at once, it was blaring at him from over his shoulder nonetheless.

Connor turned to the TV. He had no idea what was playing or why it enraged him so much. He only knew that he wanted it off. He wanted quiet. More accurately, he wanted to fully hear himself scream. He wanted to hear things break. Because, sometimes, breaking things makes a broken life feel somehow more intact.

His neighbor, hearing a pause from the destruction for a moment, decided to put her phone down. And, just as Connor was about to make his neighbor regret that choice, just as he was going to yank his thirty-two-inch flatscreen off the wall and throw it through the window, he tripped.

Fell.

He was on the floor, his world upside down around him, and he was crying. *Really* crying. The sort of crying that involves the entire body. Heaving until he felt his lungs would burst, shaking, delivering hammer fist blows to the ground as if the wall hadn't been enough of an inanimate enemy already that day. And now he wasn't thinking of nothing, though he wished he were. Now, with the blind rage subsiding and the grief taking its place, he thought of everything, his mind a burning reel of photos.

Better days. There had been better days, once upon a time.

On his side, curled into a ball and sobbing, Connor Michaels flashed back on his years like a man understanding that his life had come to an end. Because, in many ways, it had.

2

Connor thought, perhaps, that his life had ended three years prior to this afternoon as he found himself curled up and crying on his carpet. He thought his life had ended when his son had died. Then Connor had felt his life somehow end again at the funeral, a blade of ice into his heart. He had died a third time when *she* had kicked him out, ended things. Turned his daughter against him after forcing him to move into this dump. The last bit of him that had managed to survive all of those deaths expired earlier this day when he had asked his daughter for a hug goodbye, and had watched her turn and cling to her mother's leg instead.

His was repetitious death. Living was perishing in perpetuity. So many bad days. He wondered now, on this, the worst of them, if he had ever had a good one. It was hard to believe he ever had. Hard to believe that life had ever felt anything other than awful. But, as moments of his life flashed through his mind, those good days came back to him. Each sweet memory only making the bad ones to follow more devastating. He wanted to push them away, but here they were, unyielding. Playing in his head like images projected from the burning reel that was his mind.

There was the birth of his children. While both of those events were special, he thought more of his son's birth, because he thought constantly of his son's death. The brevity between the two dates – birth and death – made for frequent reflection. His boy's life was boiled down to an efficient series of a few happy moments remembered by a man who had never thought he would have to savor those memories for later.

There was the memory of hearing his son calling him 'dad-dee' for the first time. Seeing the boy's first steps and wondering where those steps would take him along the road of life, not knowing the disaster that lay ahead for his poor son. As he and his then-wife had laughed and cried joyful tears, watching their boy battle and conquer those first early foes, Gravity and Balance, how was he to know that his boy was stumbling and staggering toward an abyss. Toward an end that would leave his entire family shattered like the dishware currently on Connor's kitchen floor.

He remembered a time when he and his wife had decided to have professional photos of the two children taken – his son five and his daughter three at the time. His son had made such a fuss about sitting still for the photographer in the photobooth at the back of the department store. Such a fuss that the boy's sister had begun to cry. Only then had the young boy settled down, for the sake of his sister, and hugged her until she had done the same. The photographer had said it was the most beautiful sibling moment he had ever captured.

Another beautiful moment had been teaching his son how to ride a bike without training wheels. That had been two weeks before the accident.

He hit rewind, went back further, back before his son had been born. Back to when he had first met his wife in college. Their first date. The first time they had been intimate after weeks of going on dates while behaving as though they weren't actually dating. A friendship lost, a love born. A marriage, two children. Then devastation.

Now, the TV continued to play above and in front of Connor. It distracted him, stopped him from remembering the past while reminding him of where he presently was, of what had become of him. Connor got to his knees and was on his way to ripping the television from the wall again. Or maybe just turning it off. The sobbing had diminished his rage and need to hear things break, if only slightly. What he wanted now was silence. He longed to grab the whiskey he should have gone to in the first place. To get so deep into the bottle that he would forget what had happened today, just temporarily. What he truly wanted was to fix it all. To make it right. To—

"...relive better days?" said a voice from the television, finishing his thought but making it a question. Which is what made him look at the TV. What made him focus on it.

"Has it turned out that the present isn't the gift you expected it to be? Future not looking too bright? How about a little time off? A break, a trip down memory lane. A vacation to the good times."

It was upon hearing these words that Connor looked at the television, not just as another object to destroy but as something that captured his interest. Something that further took him away from his need to rage.

What he saw on the screen was a man wearing a red blazer, thick red rimmed glasses, and a black fedora with a red feather protruding from the side of it. The man was walking down a quaint but beautiful street. The picket fences which surrounded every front yard on that street were the color of clouds, and Connor had never seen trees look more vibrant. They were greener than anything ought to be – like the color itself was in the process of coming to life. The day displayed on the television was stunning, sun and clear skies. The place looked like a breath of fresh air after a sprint through smog. A breath of fresh air Connor could desperately use.

Connor quickly understood he was watching some sort of infomercial, though he wasn't yet certain what The Pitchman at the center of it was selling. As the red-blazered man walked down a street which resembled an exceptional piece of impressionist art, he approached a street sign. The camera zoomed in. Connor read the words **MEMORY LANE.**

When the camera zoomed out, The Pitchman was leaning against the signpost.

"If your answer was 'yes' to any of these questions, then I do believe I have what you need right here for you..." He held something between his thumb and forefinger. It was a small glass vial. The substance inside of it was a bright but cloudy blue. The Pitchman went on, "What if you could experience it all again? What if you could relive a certain time in your life, forever? Relive better days, in real time, guilt fre– "

Connor got to his feet, put his hands to the sides of the television and, after a deep breath, turned it off rather than ripping it from the wall. A small part of him knew better than to destroy it. There was no way he could afford a new television. Couldn't afford a new coffee table, or a new set of dishes. Couldn't even afford the spackle it would take to fix the holes he had made throughout his living room. He definitely couldn't afford to believe in some salesman's pitch about a substance that could open up your memory in a way that allowed you to relive your favorite days in real time. A fountain of youth you didn't have to leave your home to sip from. There was snake oil in that Pitchman's vial. That's what it boiled down to, Connor thought to himself.

He had been hearing advertisements for that product all day. Had heard the ads on nearly every radio station he had tuned into during his drive home earlier. He hadn't thought much of it at first, but the idea of the product had stayed with him even as he turned off the car radio after hearing about it one too many times.

What would he pay to relive the best days of his life? He didn't know, but the question only reminded him of all the things he couldn't afford, and the one thing he knew he could. The one thing he often wanted and knew he wouldn't have to pay for.

Suicide.

3

Suicide was free of charge and there for the taking any time he was ready. And he was feeling more ready with every passing second.

The urn. She took the fucking urn. She could have at least left me with that.

He went to his bedroom, collapsed onto his bed without bothering to remove his clothes or shoes. He grabbed the bottle of whiskey that had been waiting beside the bed for just such a moment. One of the many bottles he drank from before falling asleep at night (regardless of where in the house he happened to stumble to sleep). One of the many bottles he drank from when he woke up each morning and realized he was still alive and stuck in this existence. Regretfully so.

Would he continue on this way? Would he continue on at all? Did he truly want to? After chugging from the bottle as he lay there, Connor licked at the corner of his mouth, his tongue chasing a dribble of whiskey that had run down his stubbly cheek. He was deciding if this was the time to do it. To end it. Finally.

Along with the whiskey that had run down his cheek, so too had Connor's tears. His body was trembling again, so severely that he didn't feel the vibration of the phone in his pocket. Since arriving at home, he hadn't thought about the phone or the outside world other than his ex-wife and daughter and the ashes of his son – his old family now on their way west to start a new life. A life far away from him. One where that woman would keep poisoning his daughter against him.

His phone vibrated in his pocket again. This time he did feel it. He ignored it at first, but it refused to stop.

Connor reached into his pocket and pulled out the phone. Would have chucked it against the wall if he hadn't seen the name attached to the call he had just missed. Would have surely dashed the phone if it hadn't been his brother trying to reach him. And if he hadn't noticed that his brother had called him thirteen times in the last few hours.

Kevin – Connor's brother – had known that Connor had been planning to see his ex-wife earlier that day. Had known that Connor had been intent on going over there and begging her, one last time, not to move.

On her moving day.

With her new husband there. And possibly their family and friends as well.

Kevin had been begging him not to do it for over a week. Had told him that nothing good could come of it. And, of course, Kevin had been right.

When Connor had gotten to the house he and his ex-wife had briefly shared following the accident that killed their son, he had seen that the moving truck was not there, presumably gone. The door was open and the house seemed empty. For a heart wrenching moment he thought he was too late. That they had already left. But then he'd seen her car parked down the street and had been relieved. That relief was a short-lived feeling.

As he'd walked toward the house, she had been walking out with his daughter, Cherry, beside her. Neither had looked happy to see him. She had raised her hand, indicating for him to stop, which he did. Connor halted partway up the driveway as his ex-wife walked down the porch steps until she stood opposite him, roughly six feet away. It was the closest they had been in over a year. The closest they had been since their last day in court when he had been explicitly advised that it wouldn't be wise to be this close to his ex-wife and child for the foreseeable future. At least not without court approved supervision.

"We've been through this," said Connor's ex-wife, the former love of his life. She was the current love of his life as well. He might have admitted this out loud had anyone cared to hear it, though a statement such as that, unrequited and from a man in his position, only made him sound like a fool with an obsession.

He had tried not to wince at the severity of her voice, the sharpness of her statement. Forcing himself to smile, he had waved cheerfully to his daughter. Cherry's only response had been to look down at her tiny sandaled feet, remaining silent all the while. Connor couldn't help but to wince at that before he turned his attention back to his ex, doing his best to compose himself. He prepared to say words he had hoped would turn this from another bad day to one he could find a small victory within.

"I know, but... the urn, Becks. Can I please just have the urn?" Connor begged, sounding and feeling more pathetic than he could ever recall sounding and feeling.

"Rebecca... is everything okay?" a voice had called out from the doorway of the house. Rebecca's husband, Harold. A skinny little computer geek whose bright idea it had been to apply for a job across the country that would take Connor's family away from him. It took everything Connor had in him to not stride over the drive, walk up the porch steps and punch the stepfather to his daughter directly in his long neck. Push his jutting Adam's apple in. But Connor knew that wouldn't help. It hadn't helped the last time he had hit the man, that was for sure.

"Everything is okay, Harry. Connor just wants to say goodbye to Cherry. He seems to have forgotten that he *already did* last week like we all agreed on," Rebecca responded to her current husband without looking over her shoulder at him.

Harold stayed there in the doorway. This was the same man who had been 'just a friend' to Connor's ex-wife as she had mourned their son. A man she had met during grief-centered group therapy sessions Connor had chosen not to attend.

The 'we' Rebecca had mentioned in her statement to Harold included their family court-appointed counsellor. The counsellor who had made it so that Connor would only be allowed to see his daughter on Holidays going forward. And only under strict guidance and observation.

"I know... I just... I have nothing left, Becks. What am I gonna do without my boy?"

Rebecca bit her lower lip. Then raised her hand to her mouth and bit her knuckle instead. If their daughter hadn't been present, she might have leapt on Connor and bit into his flesh in place of lip and knuckle. Would have torn parts from him with her teeth. She had already tried to once. When she had found out the cause of their son, River's death.

Since then, she had done her best to remain calm when it came to her ex-husband, as she was doing now. She had even attempted to forgive Connor and reconcile their marriage after River's passing. For the sake of Cherry, the only child she had left. But Connor had blown that second chance by simply not trying to put his life back together. And had blown what was left of their family to pieces as a result.

"Our son is gone, Connor. Ashes won't make a difference. We've *talked* about this."

"If the ashes don't make a difference, why won't you just let me have him?" Even before the sentence had emerged from his mouth, he regretted it. Because he saw her eyes flare, her body stiffen, and her mouth open to say what they both already knew the answer was.

"Because I'm not the fuc–" She caught herself before she swore. Had looked down at her daughter who was looking up at her. Rebecca fought visibly to regain her composure. Over her left shoulder Connor could see that Harold was still at the doorway, phone in hand in case he had to call the police. Connor would have paid a great deal to have been able to headbutt that sonofabitch into unconsciousness. But, of the two men there at that moment, it was Connor who was much closer to being physically harmed than Harold. He returned his attention to his ex-wife, who said, through gritted teeth,

"I think it's only fair that I keep my son's ashes, and his urn. Since I'm not the one who put him in there."

A harpoon through his heart, that's what those words were. It wasn't the first time she had said them out loud, but it hurt no less each time they were said. And each time they were said, he had no response. There *was* no response. He had learned this the hard way.

They had stood there in silence, until Rebecca gently said,

"Conn. The urn has already been shipped to Arizona with the rest of our valuable objects. It's not here. And you shouldn't be here either."

Connor hadn't heard most of that statement. Hadn't listened to it. He was only focused on one of the several words his ex had sent his way.

Shipped.

15

She had... *shipped* his son, was what Connor had been thinking. He'd been thinking that she had shipped his son as though the boy's ashes and urn were part of a parcel of products a person could purchase online. Like he was a care package she was sending to a relative across the country. Like he was just a piece of property and nothing else.

Connor made a guttural sound in his throat. Harold flinched. Cherry hugged Rebecca's leg and pressed her face against her mother's thigh. Whimpered.

"Don't," Rebecca said abruptly. "Connor. Not today. *Not* today. We made our peace. We all said our goodbyes. We agreed. We *agreed*! Just... *please* go."

Shipped...

That's all he could think of.

His boy, who he had taught to ride a bike, who he had played catch with, who he had worked himself to the bone to provide for... shipped.

"You. *Shipped.* My son?!"

"Rebecccaaaaaaa?" Harold said nervously from the doorway, his finger hovering over the screen of his phone, as if he had already pressed nine and one and was waiting for a reason to finalize the number. Rebecca ignored Harold, keeping her eyes on her fuming ex-husband the way a lion tamer would when approaching an ornery big cat. She knew she could handle him, always had been able to. But that didn't make the potential for danger any less likely.

"Connor," Rebecca had said. Slowly. Cautiously. Every word a careful choice. "I have *begged* Harold not to call the police on you, because I know that your life will be ruined if you get arrested again. I don't want that for you, because, believe it or not, I do still care. But we're moving. *Literally* moving on. We sent the remains of our son with great care ahead of us, and I'm tracking the sh... the progress the entire time. I loved – *love* – River just as much as you do, and I would hope that you aren't suggesting that I would do anything to disrespect him or his remains."

Lion tamed. He could say nothing to that. Again, they only stared at one another as Harold's finger hovered closer to his phone, and Connor's daughter began to visibly tremble. Eventually, he thought of the living child he had, realizing that he couldn't part ways with her like this. They'd had an awkward but peaceful visit the week before. He was beginning to realize he should have left it at that. Not bothering to respond to Rebecca, Connor turned to his daughter.

"Cherry?" he'd said carefully, but she wouldn't return his look. She almost had, for a moment. Had peeked up from her mother's leg. But before their eyes could meet, just as he had opened his arms for a hug, she had turned her eyes away, turned her body back toward Rebecca. Clung to her mother's leg instead.

Neither of the women he considered to be his family could stand to look at him. He stared at the back of the head of his child as she held on to his disgruntled ex-wife. Then his eyes had focused on the crown of his ex-wife's head as she had stooped down to comfort their distressed daughter.

Four eyes, healthy and available, and not a single one would lock upon his two. Connor looked up and saw that not even Harold would look directly at the scene.

His eyes drifted back to his daughter's head. Most of the hair there was hers now. Beneath her hair, the back of her neck bore horrific scars. Also Connor's fault. He had always been glad those scars hadn't reached her face. A face she couldn't bring herself to show to him.

"Okay..." he had said shakily. Rage and hurt and uncertainty making his body quiver, making his brow gleam with sweat despite the cool late-summer afternoon.

"Okay…" he said again. Then, knowing that nothing was okay, but not knowing what else to say, he had turned and walked, still quaking with anger, toward his vehicle.

"You'll see her at Thanksgiving, Conn!" Rebecca had called out. He ignored her.

"Connor? You haven't been drinking, have you?" He continued to rage walk away, saying nothing.

"Are you okay to drive?" He hated when she talked about his drinking. Not responding, he began to jog the rest of the way to his car – a rusted and old and embarrassing vehicle. A car almost comically small for a man as tall and broad as he.

"Please take care of yourself!" was the last of what Rebecca had yelled to Connor as he had reached his car. He said nothing in return. Got in. Drove off.

The next thing he remembered was foul tasting water.

Connor was going over his day once more, bed beneath him, whiskey burning his throat. Going over everything that had led up to this day, and everything he could remember from this day that had led up to this moment. His morose memories were only interrupted when the phone in his hand began to vibrate again.

4

Connor felt the vibration of his phone, knew who it was. Confirmed this knowledge when he looked at his mobile device and saw that it was Kevin, his brother, trying to reach him now for the fourteenth time.

He saw from the icon on his phone that he already had half a dozen voice messages. And because he didn't want to have to check half a dozen more, he clicked the green button.

"Not a great time, Kev," he croaked out. He had been hoping to sound normal but his voice sounded as terrible as he felt.

"Fuck. Connor. Did you actually go there?"

"Not a great time, Kev," he repeated more certainly after clearing his throat. He hated when people spoke to him the way his brother was speaking to him now. In hushed tones, sad whispers. In a soft sort of way meant to convey empathy, sympathy, something that irritated Connor to no end. These days people spoke to him as though it were his eardrums that were damaged and not his life. It was difficult when he got it from old friends and acquaintances – those still willing to speak to him – after they found out what his life had become. But it was nearly unbearable when it came from his little brother, who had, at some point in their lives, become the older brother in every way but chronologically.

Kevin had a great job, a wonderful house, and a beautiful wife he had been with since his senior year of high school. The couple had young, healthy, living children who loved them and were able to make eye contact with both parents without looking somewhere for help. They had a family that hadn't been broken by misfortune.

An accident, Connor told himself. For a time beyond count, he said internally: *just a mistake.*

To his brother, he said nothing. And for a time they simply listened to one another breathe.

"Okay, okay. I'll swing by in a few days. Things will get better, I promise..." When Connor didn't respond, his brother, who was younger by only ten months, said, "Remember *your* promise, Connor. I need my big brother."

"Yeah, I remember. Don't worry." He hung up the phone. If he had said more, he would have broken down again. He didn't want that. Wasn't sure if he or his house could survive another emotional outburst. And if he didn't survive, then he would be breaking his word to Kevin.

Connor had promised his brother, not long after River's death, that he wouldn't kill himself. Not while Kevin was still alive. Their dad was many years gone, and Connor hadn't communicated with their mother in years. He often said the two brothers only had each other, though he knew the truth was that Kevin had many others. He had a loving marriage, three beautiful kids, and a decent social life in addition to a burden of a brother.

Kevin had known what Connor had in mind not long after the accident. He had guilted his older brother into promising not to take his own life. Connor resented that promise at times like this. Truly did. But no one loved him like his brother did. He didn't believe anyone else loved him at all. Connor had disappointed his loved ones and former supporters with the life he had led. He didn't want the end of this letdown of a life to be a final disappointment to the only person who cared about him. So long as he stayed breathing, he knew he wouldn't be letting at least one person down. It was all he held on to.

What he no longer wanted to hold on to was his phone. He was about to put it away when he saw an unfamiliar icon on his screen. A notification he didn't recognize.

The icon appeared to be an outline of a black, forward-facing fedora with a red feather sticking out of its left side. Beneath the hat was another outline, in red, of a sideways number 8. Infinity, he thought. Though when he looked closer, he saw that what he had taken to be an infinity symbol was only a pair of glasses. The same red rimmed glasses the man on the television had been wearing. The Pitchman. This icon was an illustration of that same man. The wording beneath it said:

LIVAGAIN

Connor remembered what the man on the radio and television advertisements had said. About being able to relive a certain time in your life over. It had sounded so good. Too good to be true. He knew that, rationally. And he knew he couldn't afford it even if it were true.

Connor took a swallow from the bottle of whiskey. Cheap whiskey, the burning in his throat reminded him. He was a broke loser, he reminded himself after considering clicking on the icon of the black fedora.

Connor took another swig.

No wife, no kids, no life. Nothing, he told himself.

He drank one final deep gulp before he closed the bottle and went to set it on the floor beside the bed. It fell with a clang. He let it roll beneath the bed, not bothering to reach for it, to set it right. He deserved to crawl for the bottle the next time he wanted a drink, is what he thought while still gazing at the black fedora. Thinking of better days.

The icon was becoming hazy, his vision becoming blurred.

He didn't click on the notification on his phone. Instead, he let the device fall beside him on the bed. He closed his eyes. Passed out.

5

Connor was walking. That in itself was a surprise. He couldn't remember the last time he had walked anywhere, but he was walking now. Along an empty street, underneath a cloudless sky that was too blue. The wrong shade of the color. It looked to Connor as though an ocean had risen, a tsunami suspended in the sky above him. It was as beautiful as it was unsettling.

Struggling to remove his eyes from the strange sky, Connor continued this rare walk down a familiar looking street. Though it was a street he was sure he had never seen before. Not up close and in person.

He walked for several uncertain steps toward the minor intersection up ahead as he looked up at the street signs to see just where he was.

MEMORY LANE and **MEMORY LANE**.

He remembered now where he had seen this place before. Facing north, he saw the lovely picket-fenced street The Pitchman had been walking down in the infomercial on his television. He looked west and saw a street that was remarkably similar. He checked back north, then west again, comparing each house, looking at the cracks in the road, the speed bumps, the sewer lids. The absence of a single car in any of the driveways.

They weren't just similar streets. They were identical.

He turned east. Made the same observations. Also identical. South was literally no different than the other three directions.

Understanding that all choices were one choice, Connor, somehow, all at the same time, travelled north, east, south and west as he walked along Memory Lane.

The first thing he noticed about the houses, aside from the fact that they were all identical cottage style homes, was that none of them had curtains, nor drapes, nor blinds. There wasn't a covered window in the neighborhood. The second thing he noticed, and very quickly, was that each house was his, though not literally.

These weren't houses that looked like his current home or the modest two-bedroom bungalow his family had lived in when he was a young boy. Nor did they resemble even slightly the large townhouse his family had moved into when Connor was eight, after his father had gotten the huge promotion he had waited his entire life for, only to have a heart attack and die the next year. None of these houses was the dorm he had stayed in during college. Or any of the places he had moved into afterward with his college sweetheart and now ex-wife, Rebecca. But every time he looked into the curtain-less windows of each of these identical homes, he saw a scene from some point in his past. Something wonderful that had been buried deep in his mind by both the years and the bad experiences those years had brought with them.

In one house he saw his parents and his brother, all sitting together at the dinner table with him – a much younger version of him. A version he barely recognized. As amazed as he was by the sight of his childhood self, he was far more fascinated by the sight of his father, awed to see the man animated and not just a still shot in a photo to be mourned and reminisced over.

There was a birthday cake in front of the young version of himself inside of that house. On it were five candles. On five-year-old Connor's face was a grin so wide it seemed as if the corners of his lips might touch his ears. *When last did I smile like that?* he wondered. Then a follow-up: *When last did I smile at all?*

He peered into the next house, through large bay windows, understanding that he should have been looking at a living room or maybe a kitchen. Instead, he saw his childhood bedroom.

Inside of the bedroom, looking as it had roughly five years after he had blown the candles on that birthday cake out, he saw a bunkbed. Saw himself on the top bunk, Kevin on the bottom. On the floor in sleeping bags were their two respective best friends, Jimmy and Michael. The four had been nearly inseparable for years. Then life happened. Puberty, girls, new interests outside of comic books and running around for the sake of running around. Sex. Adulthood. Life. Now Connor wasn't even certain if the two were still alive. And if they were alive, he had no idea where they were living. But that didn't matter, they were here and right in front of him in this moment.

Connor almost smiled as he looked into the room and remembered that epic sleepover. They had tried to 'break the night' by staying up until the sun rose. It would have been the fifth time they had tried to make it until sunrise that summer. Each previous time, they had talked and had fun, and had also failed. But on this occasion, they had made it all the way. Even though they were dead tired for all of the next day, none of them had regretted it when Connor's mom had woken them up only two hours after the last of the boys had fallen asleep, dozing off while talking about who would win in a no rules street fight between Batman and Wolverine. That night had somehow made that entire summer perfect. Now, with his life full of sleepless nights, it was hard to imagine how staying up until dawn could equate to happiness. Yet he was seeing it, remembering it as it played out in front of him.

He continued his stroll down Memory Lane.

There were scenes from several moments of his life playing inside of each of the identical cottage style homes that lined the wide street of Memory Lane. In one home was the scene of the first time he and Rebecca had had sex. It was the kitchen of his college house that he was looking at inside of this home. He, Rebecca and several others had come back from a night out at a local bar. Everyone had stayed up drinking until it was only the two of them, staying up, still drinking. And while several of their roommates and classmates (and at least one random) were passed out in the living room, Connor and Rebecca were just feet away, her ass on top of a pair of pizza boxes to get her to the right level, him between her legs.

Heaven had been that kitchen on that drunk and blurry night.

The next house was truly inexplicable. Inside the window, where Connor had imagined a living area would be, was green grass. A football field stretched through the interior of the house. A football field at the center of a stadium. Yet the house itself was no bigger than any other on the lane.

Connor could see an entire game going on in there. On a field 120 yards long from endzone to endzone, and 53.5 yards wide from sideline to sideline. Green gridiron at the center of a stadium full of students, alumni, boosters, fans. People all rooting for the hometown team. And the soon-to-be-crowned hero: a young sophomore named Connor Michaels.

This was the scene of his first game as quarterback for his college. An NCAA school, a nationally televised game, three touchdowns thrown in the second half after he had entered as a replacement for the injured starter. Triumph from what had looked like certain defeat. The world was his after that game, he remembered thinking. Recalled believing that this was just the start. The adoration, the gifts, the girls, the women. It was supposed to be only the beginning. At least that's what his coach, the media, the country had said. And that's what he had believed. Had been certain his future would be a wonderland. If he had only known.

In another house down the lane, Connor saw that a couple had just walked into the living room, the woman carrying a baby boy. He barely recognized the couple. It was him and Rebecca, and they looked so different because they were happy. Happy, these days, to Connor, seemed like a stranger long forgotten. But he almost felt it here and now, wherever and whenever this was, outside on the sidewalk as he looked into the house that contained this memory.

Usually, all thoughts of his son brought about guilt, pain, hurt. Whiskey. But he was happy seeing the little boy's face. Felt no rage and had no urge to drink. It was a beautiful memory, pure in and of itself.

"It can always be this way, you know."

The voice came out of nowhere, and everywhere, and immediately to Connor's right. He nearly gave himself whiplash with how quickly he turned to look at the source. To look at what he'd been certain had been an empty street.

But now, right in the middle of that previously empty two-way road, close to where Memory Lane seemed to be coming to an end, was an old-fashioned kiosk that reminded Connor of a carnival ticket booth. Though instead of candy cane red and white, the wood of the booth was painted black all over. There was a hand-painted sign on the front of it, below the window facing Connor. In brilliant blue, the same as the ocean-like sky above, was the word:

LIVAGAIN

Inside of the Kiosk, looking out and at Connor from the open entry of the little wooden hut, a wide smile on his face, was The Pitchman.

6

The Pitchman was dressed the same as he had been in the infomercial. He wore a red blazer over black pants and a black collared shirt. Keeping the collar of that shirt together was a red and black bowtie. On his head was his black fedora, a bright red feather jutting from its side. Beneath that hat, cobalt-colored eyes peered at Connor from behind red frames. Those eyes shone, as did the smile, when The Pitchman noticed that Connor had noticed him.

"Has it turned out that the present isn't the gift you expected it to be? Future not looking too bright? How about a little time off? A break, a trip down memory lane. A vacation to the good times." His voice was up-tempo and tinny. It sounded, to Connor's ears, like an old recording playing at 1.5 times its normal speed. And when he looked at the man's lips as he talked, Connor noticed that the words which came out of them were out of sync with the movements they made. Off by only a fraction of a second. That fraction of a second was enough to make Connor feel slightly dizzy as he observed The Pitchman speaking. Connor wanted to look away but found that he couldn't. Something about the man was mesmerizing.

Then, thankfully, he stopped speaking, though he never stopped smiling. And that smile itself, even without the discordant words from behind it, was still disorienting. His lips were a nearly too-pink shade against the pale canvas of his face. When he smiled widely it looked as though an artist was extending those pink lips with delicate brushstrokes. Watching the man in motion was like witnessing sentient art.

Just as he had in the infomercial, The Pitchman produced a vial full of a cloudy blue substance and displayed it to Connor.

"It can always be this way, you know."

The booth was still half a block away, but Connor could hear and see the man as though he were right in front of him. He looked at the glass container of blue liquid, looked at those red rimmed glasses, and decided, even here in what he now understood had to be a dream, he didn't believe he could afford the cost of that medicine. Not at the price that a man like this might demand.

Which is why he turned around to walk away from The Pitchman and his wares. But, before he could take a step away, he saw that the old wooden kiosk with the fresh coat of black paint was in the middle of the street in that direction as well. It was in front of him again, even though he had turned his back to it.

And so was The Pitchman, blue vial in hand.

"I do believe I have what you need right here for you. What if you could experience it all again? What if you could relive a certain time in your life forever..."

"I... I'm not interested," Connor called out. He turned back in the direction he had been walking originally, and nearly screamed after doing so.

The Pitchman was right there in front of him. That is to say, he had been right there behind Connor, startling him badly when Connor had turned around.

The shock caused Connor to fall to the ground, landing on his hands and haunches. Nervously, he looked back and forth in both directions along the road. The street was clear, the black kiosk was gone. But the Pitchman was still there.

He hovered over Connor, the brim of his Fedora partially shading his face. His lips parted as he smiled, exposing teeth which were vibrant and sparkling white, shining out beneath the shadow created by his hat.

"Can I interest you in better days?" The Pitchman asked, the tempo and tone of his voice like a calming touch. A soothing breeze.

"I... What is this?" Connor responded, indicating everything around them.

"Why, it's Memory Lane! A place you can visit anytime you wish to. Here you'll find all of the best memories you've ever had with none of the sadness that comes along with them. The good without the residue of regret. All you have to do is look into a window, pick a memory you like, walk through the accompanying door, and you're there again. Reliving that magical moment in real time!"

"I can't afford it..." Connor sputtered before adding, with growing trepidation, a tremble in his voice, "And I don't believe it."

"You can and you do! Because you have seen it and seeing is believing! However, much like the cost of your trip down Memory Lane, *talk* is cheap. Imagine being able to walk through each of these doors and experiencing any one of your many amazing memories any time you want. Completely at your leisure!"

As he said this, he extended his hand behind him like a docent presenting to Connor the featured exhibit of a museum. All at once the street that looked like it had been coming to an end only a half block away lengthened. Grew. Instantly, the road seemed to stretch endlessly into the horizon. On both sides of it were miles of cottage style houses with white picket fences around them. Each one, Connor understood, contained a special memory of his.

Each one waiting for him to walk in, to relive some part of his life that hadn't been dominated by bad days.

He thought back to he and Rebecca on the kitchen counter of his college house. The young man who had spent so much time between her soft but strong legs had no idea how much pain that bit of pleasure was leading the two of them toward. Oh, to be that ignorant again!

Was there really a price that could be placed on a feeling such as that?

Or to go back into the house which had contained that epic all-night sleepover. What would he pay to remember fully all they had discussed for those many defiant hours they had stayed up between bedtime and sunrise with only their voices in the dark as entertainment? He would love to be able to recall which girls they had been crushing on, the books they had been reading, the athletes and superheroes they had wanted to be. None of them knowing that life didn't care for their hopes and expectations. That the future itself was a bitter, brazen beast ready to blindside and bludgeon them whenever it had the chance. He would love nothing more than the opportunity to relive a time before he had mourned his son, or his father. Before he knew what mourning was.

Innocence. What was the cost of an injection of that? How much would he spend for a sip of those sublime scenes.

Still, he knew he couldn't afford it.

"We do have payment plans, you know. Something we can work out over time."

"What exactly do you mean?" Connor got himself back to his feet and looked over the shoulder of The Pitchman. The street seemed to stretch even further now. Thousands and thousands of wonderful pain-free memories. Did he have that many good memories? He would never have believed so, but he would never have remembered many of the wonderful things he had been allowed to see through those open windows so fa–

Connor did a double take. Then a triple and quadruple as he saw that all of the windows of every house had become draped or blinded in the time it took to blink. Each was covered in some way to prevent Connor from being able to see inside.

Free trial's over, he thought to himself. Seeing all of those draped over windows hurt Connor in a way he could not previously have imagined. Each one a pin pressed slowly into his heart. As Connor lamented, The Pitchman said,

"Over time. A payment plan." Then The Pitchman held out his hand, not the hand containing the cloudy blue vial, but the empty one. He held it palm up, waiting for it to be filled.

Connor wasn't sure what to do, though he didn't have much time to think things over because suddenly his pants began to sag. He wasn't wearing a belt on his jeans, and they were being weighed down, slipping off, threatening to leave him exposed in the street. There was something in his right pocket. Something heavy that hadn't been inside of it only a second prior.

He reached into his pocket for what was weighing down his jeans and clutched what felt like the top of a large cylinder that could not possibly have been there before. It was something he was certain he had never previously touched. Because the sensation it gave him as his fingers first found it was unforgettable. It was solid, but it pulsed. It had a beat that matched the rhythm of his heart. The object sent waves, almost a vibration, through his body that left him feeling unsettled. He removed it from his pocket. Stared at it in shock, in awe.

It wasn't a cylinder but an ornate hourglass, about the size of a can of soda. Its heft made it feel like he was holding a brick.

The framing around the glass seemed to have been carved out of black stone with veins of red running through it, like lava flowing through ash. The glass portion of the object didn't look like the typical hourglass. It was shaped distinctly like the number 8. And, inside of it, blue sand had begun to fall from the top half to the bottom. Filling it there, ticking time away with each falling grain.

Connor looked at it, wondered where it could have come from. It felt heavy and hot in his hand. Too hot. Too heavy. And it never stopped pulsing. Its revelation inspired the rise of an unnerving feeling within him, causing him to want it out of his hand as quickly as possible. Without thinking, Connor passed the Timepiece over to The Pitchman, who took it with a smile. The expression looked as though it belonged to a creature capable of devouring flesh without needing to clean or cook it first.

"Looks like we have a deal!" said The Pitchman. He placed the Timepiece into the interior breast pocket of his jacket. From the same pocket, he produced a large item that – much like the Timepiece – should not have been able to fit comfortably into his blazer without it being noticeable. Yet, somehow, Connor hadn't noticed it. This new object was atypical in its shape and appearance, but he instantly recognized it for what it was.

It was a doorknob.

Like the Timepiece, it was also black as jet and veined with red. And, like the Timepiece, it too was shaped like a figure eight. It had three red gems inside of it – two in the top half of the eight, and one in the bottom. The Pitchman was holding the doorless knob out in the direction of Connor. Connor believed he was doing this in order to show him the ornate design. Perhaps this was part of their payment plan. He believed that until The Pitchman let go of the doorknob and stepped away from it.

Connor instinctively looked to the ground, where he considered diving to in order to catch the beautiful and very valuable looking doorknob before it dropped. But it didn't.

It didn't drop.

The doorknob floated there, in the air, roughly at waist level to Connor. Though it never fell, Connor nearly did when he noted, then registered, that it hadn't. He nearly fell again as, all at once, what looked to be twisted, leafless tree branches and gnarled stretches of root began to sprout from the sides of the knob. Connor watched in wonder as the emerging wood tentacled in every direction, stretched, hung there momentarily like a small-bodied, many-legged beast, before it filled out and took on the dimensions of a door. Then it smoothened itself out until it became one. One of the many identical cherrywood doors that led into each of the houses here on Memory Lane. It stood there in the street, defying reason and logic like the rest of this wherever-this-was that surrounded them.

In the middle of this door was an oval pane of frosted glass. Beyond the pane of glass – where Connor should have seen the figure of The Pitchman, who stood on the other side of the door – he thought he saw shades of his past. Shapes of those who had been part of his life during the better days he now physically ached to revisit. He was desperate to see them in full flesh. In real time, as The Pitchman had promised.

The Pitchman walked around his side of the freestanding door that would have brought traffic to ruin had there been a single car upon this Endless Road. He walked over until he was by Connor's side. Once there, he gestured dramatically for Connor to open the door. A door upon which Connor had placed his hand without hesitation. Because those shades of his past – those good times, pain free – were things he wanted to see again. To experience once more. To relive. Badly beyond words.

He ran his hand along the door, as if needing to feel it in order to believe that it was there. Ran his hand down the door until it found the ornate knob. Twisted it and opened up the entryway.

At the same time, in unison, each identical door to each identical house along Memory Lane (which somehow ran north and south and east and west all at once) swung open. Every blissful memory Connor Michaels ever had danced inside those homes. They called to him, the doors a thousand mouths beckoning. To come. To enter. To live again.

But, inside of the door immediately in front of him, he was surprised to see a place he didn't want to go. A place that held memories that weren't pleasant. Memories that were all pain.

"You have successfully placed your order! Your item will be delivered within twenty-four hours!" The Pitchman said this in a voice that suddenly sounded not only tinny and up-tempo, but outright mechanical.

When Connor hesitated, The Pitchman gently patted his own chest. A reminder that the breast pocket of his blazer, although flat, held a blue-sanded Timepiece. One which was counting down. *Don't forget our deal*, is what the gesture implied.

Connor looked around at all the open doors, knowing he could get back to them once his item was delivered. But also knowing that he had to face this one unbearable place first.

As he walked through the free-standing door, he heard The Pitchman say,

"Take caution, friend! Memory Lane is a long stretch of Road. When you come back, careful you don't get lost!"

Connor, not certain how to respond, simply closed the door behind him.

7

Connor woke up walking. His body wasn't actually moving anywhere, but it was trying to. Trying to move forward, only to find itself impeded.

His nose hurt, his knees were hitting and sliding against something, and his forehead was sore. He was in the corner of a room, periodically trying to walk his way through the walls.

When he came to full consciousness, he stopped his legs from moving and removed his face from the wedge between the two walls in front of him.

Sleepwalking again, he thought.

Sleepwalking was something Connor did when he was truly stressed. He had been diagnosed with somnambulism shortly after the death of his son. Add to that his bouts of insomnia, and he was a man who could be in motion for twenty-four hours of the day, even in the few hours when he slept. It wasn't a fun condition to deal with at the best of times. It was worse when one was alone and prone to doing any number of dangerous things while stumbling around asleep.

He turned from the wall and nearly fell when he saw the scene in front of him. He wished he could turn back around and ignore it. Wished he could walk through the wall and keep on walking.

He was looking at his living room.

Or what remained of it.

His couch was upside down, the cushions nowhere near it. The coffee table would never hold a cup of coffee again, its legs removed forcefully from it. Along with his pair of dollar store paintings, the wall across from him was full of holes, most the size of his fists. Holes that would require many more dollar store paintings to cover them.

Papers, pamphlets, takeout menus were all over the floor. Fragments of plates that should have been fused together in one piece and placed neatly in the kitchen cabinets had somehow found their way into the living room, as had several items that should have been in the fridge. Connor had no memory of throwing what looked to be a shattered bottle of pickles from the kitchen into this area, but he often forgot specific details of his day when in the depths of a bright red rage. Looking at the area around him, he felt another bout of the red rage rising. He went to ball his hands into fists. Found instead that one of his hands was clasped around something. He had apparently grabbed his phone before somnambulating his way out of bed.

He looked down at it. The screen was still unlocked.

The first thing he noticed was the time. 3:05 AM.

He couldn't recall when he had crashed. He knew he had made it to his bed. He remembered talking to Kevin. But it was all blurry.

The second thing he noticed, in the middle of the screen, were the words:

You have successfully placed your order!
Your item will be delivered within 24 hours!

It was an alert from a website he had never before been to, though the name of it flirted with his memory. LIVAGAIN.COM.

"God. Damn. It!" Connor enunciated, seething through clenched teeth. He couldn't afford any order of any item.

Not caring what the item was that he had ordered while walking in his sleep, he went to find an option to cancel it but could find none. Just as he was about to hurl his phone in frustration, he looked around the living room again. He already had enough to clean up as it was, he warned himself. Connor took a deep breath instead of flinging the phone. Decided the bottle of whiskey was the better option for the time being. He planned to call the company he felt had taken advantage of him by tricking him into buying their product while he slept. He would be sure to give them a piece of his mind later in the day, after sleeping properly.

Taking careful steps to avoid the mess all over the floor, Connor made his way back to his bedroom. Eventually, after crawling to retrieve his whiskey bottle from beneath his bed and damning himself all the while, he managed to sleep horizontally for the remainder of the night.

8

Connor woke up to the ringing of a bell. His doorbell. He looked at his phone to check the time, blinking most of the haze from his eyes. He thought, for a confusing second, that the time read 8:88. He blinked away more haze. Saw that it was 8:08 AM.

It was Monday morning and Connor was supposed to be at work at the recycling plant for his afternoon shift by 1 PM. It was a job he hated, but his brother had helped him get it, making him feel obligated to go there for more than monetary reasons. Still, his shift – which involved standing next to a conveyor belt while separating trash from recyclable products for a third of his day – was five hours off. He wanted to dedicate several of those five hours to getting more rest. But the doorbell rang again. He felt his red rage rising even before he fully woke.

She took the fucking urn, and now I can't even get a few Goddamned hours of sleep!

Connor thought of all the knives in his kitchen. They could help him sleep a while. Then he remembered the promise he had made to his little brother and only friend. He did his best to dim the red in his head.

Once he had found some small measure of composure, he staggered his way to the front door, body sore, head aching from the whiskey, eyes still somewhat cloudy, mind still everywhere but here. He wondered if, at this very moment, Rebecca and that fucking asshole of a husband of hers were getting settled into their nice new home after unpacking the ashes of his son, which they had *shipped* ahead of them. Connor's mind was not a pleasant place.

The bell rang again as his hand touched the door to open it. He took small pleasure in knowing that he was going to unleash all of the remaining red in his mind onto whoever it was that was poking the shit out of his doorbell.

Connor swung the door open violently, not caring that the movement caused a sharp burst of pain to travel through his head. He was ready to cause significantly more pain to whoever it was insisting on ringing his doorbell incessantly when it was barely after sunrise.

He had his mouth in motion, preparing to spew fire from it, ready to chew somebody's – anybody's – head off. But when he saw what was out there on the other side of the open doorway, his mouth stilled from shock.

No one was there.

"Goddamned fucking kids wanna play ding dong ditch on me? I'll put your little narrow ass in a Goddamned ding dong ditch!" Connor growled. He dashed out of the house, still in the shoes he had worn to sleep, determined to catch the person who had woken him up. Whoever was trying to prank Connor, that person would pay. He swore that to himself as he sprinted out of his home. But, when he got to the end of his driveway and looked in both directions down the sidewalk, he saw no one. He waited, thinking maybe someone would slip up and come creeping out from behind a bush or around some corner, but no one did.

"No one could have gotten away that fast," he muttered to himself. Confused, Connor walked back toward his house.

And that's when he saw it.

His purchase, the item that was supposed to arrive within twenty-four hours, had been delivered in five. It was directly in front of his door, leaning against the single cement step that led to his rundown bungalow.

How could I have missed that? he wondered. Then he knew. It was rage. His anger had been blinding him for some time now.

Not quite sure what he was moving toward, and a bit nervous as he did so, Connor walked slowly and uncertainly to the small brown package which was no larger than a box of tissue paper.

On the label of the package was a red sticker with the words **FOR CONNOR** written on it in bold black print. Beneath those words was a graphic. The logo of the company he had ordered this item from while he slept:

The words **8 MEMORY LANE, OMNITOWN** were stamped on the box. The address of the sender.

Omnitown? He hadn't heard of it. The return address didn't include a country, which made Connor wonder if this was some of that mystical Chinese medicine he had heard of his entire life. With the strange herbs and crushed rhino horn and pangolin scales and all sorts of ingredients that Connor had no interest in. If he wasn't going to give his money over to an American company, there was no way he was going to pay the extra cost of having this thing shipped from somewhere across the ocean. Or the cost of whatever rare or near-extinct thing that had been plucked or butchered for this purpose.

He picked up the package and thought to march right to the post office and send it back to Omnitown, wherever in the world that was. Instead, he decided to take it into his house while he used his phone to check his bank account and transaction records. He braced himself for the blow that would be the cost of the item inside of this package.

When he accessed his account, he was surprised. Genuinely shocked. Not by the amount he had paid but by the fact that no amount had been paid at all. The last twenty transactions on his account were from the liquor store, fast food restaurants, or gas stations. Nothing from LIVAGAIN. He looked back at the box in his hand as though it would have some answer for him, and was pleased to find that it did. Stamped on one of the sides of the box were the words:

FREE TRIAL SAMPLE

Okay, he thought. *Free,* he thought. *I can handle that.*

Connor opened the box, removed a folded piece of paper from the top to see the more interesting item beneath it.

Surrounded by a layer of protective black Styrofoam was a glass vial with a chrome lid. Inside of it was a hazy but bright blue liquid, the sight of which placed into Connor's mind the preposterous thought of a blue cloud somehow being plucked from the sky, collected and bottled. The vial was roughly the size of a bottle of nail polish and looked like something he might have found in a science lab. It looked just like the one The Pitchman had held in the commercial he had seen on the television, he now recalled.

Connor wasn't sure what to do, whether to consume the blue liquid or not. He unfolded the paper that had been in the box. On it was a description of the effects and side effects of the blue substance:

BEGINS WORKING IMMEDIATELY

For mental and physical rejuvenation through ALL-NATURAL hippocampal stimulation via the optic nerve.

Simply focus on a memory, place a drop of MEMLAIN-8 (The Mental Health Fixer Elixir!) in each eye, and you can relive a better day
IN REAL TIME!

Side Effects: Mild disorientation, loss of appetite, a sense of Disreality, drowsiness, and deep muscle relaxation.

DO NOT USE WHILE OPERATING HEAVY MACHINERY!

Would he use it at all? Connor wasn't sure. He turned the paper over, looking for a list of the supposedly all-natural ingredients used to make this cloudy blue substance. He found none. He had assumed the liquid was for drinking, but after reading the instructions and taking a closer look at the bottle, Connor realized that what he held in his hand was a glass eyedropper.

He read the side effects again, and actually liked the way most of them sounded. He could use some mild disorientation. He didn't know what Disreality was, but it had to be better than this reality, he thought. Considering he felt like he hadn't slept at all, a bit of drowsiness and muscle relaxation couldn't hurt. Would be downright pleasant after what he had put his body through with yesterday's tantrum. Even the lack of appetite would help Connor out presently. He could barely afford food these days. And, thinking of the state of his kitchen, he realized he no longer had plates on which to eat whatever food he could afford.

No, he didn't want to deal with the cleanup, the remorse, the reliving of *those* sorts of memories. MEMLAIN-8 sounded perfect just now.

What could be the harm in giving it a shot?

He collected the box and the instruction paper, and made his way through the wreckage of his house to his bathroom.

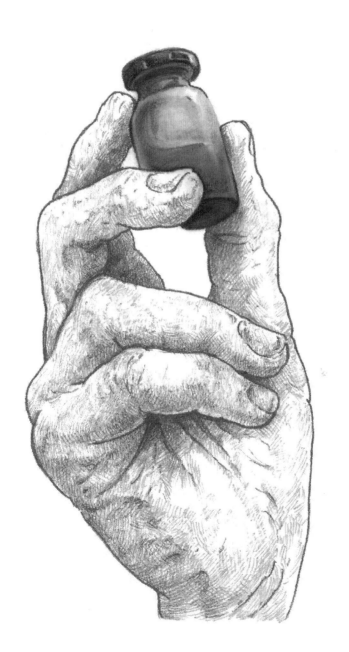

9

Connor didn't know what he expected to feel when he took the dropper out of its bottle and carefully placed a single drop of the viscous blue liquid into his left eye (the eye he was willing to sacrifice first, he supposed, if things went wrong). He was glad the first feeling he felt was relief after waiting for a second or two and not feeling any burning or stinging. Another several seconds, nearly a minute, and he decided it was safe to place a drop into his other eye. Then he waited some more for this supposed immediate reaction.

He felt nothing as he stared into the mirror, looking at an aging face belonging to a broken man who appeared nearly ten years older than the thirty-nine years he was.

No reaction.

Nothing. Just like what remained in the cabinets in the kitchen. Just like him, his life, what he had amounted to. Nothing. He was about to say the word 'bullshit' and dump the vial in the trash, until he remembered what he hadn't been remembering, which was to remember.

The instructions had told him to focus on a positive memory from his past, and here he was letting his present beat him up again. Though now that it came time to remember, Connor had no clue which memory to go to. He could find a thousand bad ones, but a good one? That was a challenge.

Suddenly, and for no reason he could understand, a memory came to mind. It was of himself as a kid, on a night when he, his brother, and two of their friends, Michael and Jimmy, had 'broken the night' and stayed up until sunrise. That had been a good memory for sure. One of the best.

Connor was surprised to see, just then, in the mirror, that he was smiling. The expression so foreign to him that he was genuinely startled. It looked like a stranger was staring back at him. A man he didn't recognize. The smile didn't stay on his face for long, however, because in the mirror was another surprise: his hazel eyes were turning blue.

"Hooooly fuck!" he said as he stumbled backward until he hit the closed bathroom door. His bathrobe and the towel that hung from the door softened the blow. "What the..." He took a few shuddering steps toward the mirror, opened his eyes wide. Yes, his irises were now the same cobalt color as the MEMLAIN-8.

"*That* is fucking cool!"

He stared into the mirror a while longer, waiting for something else to happen, something associated with the memory from that day, but he felt no different. Not drowsy, not disoriented. He went to turn, to exit the bathroom and head to his bedroom. He was in the middle of saying, "Maybe I just have to wait a bit longer for it to kick in" when he realized that things were not as they should have been.

By the time he had turned to face the door, he was no longer in his bathroom. Well, technically speaking, he *was* in his bathroom. Though it wasn't the bathroom he had been standing in moments before.

Connor looked around, bewildered and befuddled (there was the disorientation), at the Timon and Pumbaa shower curtains dividing the bathtub from the rest of the lavatory. There were images on the towels hanging from the rack on the door as well. Towels that did not belong to him. At least not anymore. Not for decades now.

Connor, very cautiously, extremely slowly, reached out to touch the towels, as if afraid they would turn to ash in his hands if he didn't handle them with the utmost care. First the Teenage Mutant Ninja Turtles towel that had belonged to Kevin when they were kids, and then, just as carefully, he fingered the nearly threadbare towel beside it. On this towel was the Millennium Falcon from Star Wars, drifting through space. Connor remembered using that thing until it was in tatters, refusing to let go of it. Only to find that his mother had one day thrown it away in secret. He had been unreasonably upset about that back then as a child, but the memory of it made him smile here and now.

Where am I? he wondered. He felt like he was inside of his childhood home, but that couldn't be. Not truly. He thought back to the listed effects of the substance, reminded himself that this was just a vivid remembrance, some sort of 'all-natural' hallucin–

There was a knock on the door.

Holy Jesus! he thought to himself before stumbling backward onto the toilet bowl. He nearly fell over it, through the curtain and into the tub. But he was able to right himself before he did so.

"Connor?" a voice said through the door.

It was the voice of a young child.

Whispering,

"Connor?"

Connor didn't know what to say. His heart was hammering in his chest. His throat was tight. He most definitely did not feel deeply relaxed.

The knock again. Then the voice whispering harshly,

"Holy shit, dude. Do you have explosive diarrhea in there? I need to take a leeeeeeeeak!"

And that was when Connor remembered this part of this night.

"One sec!" he said, without even realizing he had intended to say it. He nearly fell over again when he heard that his own voice now sounded like that of a child. Like that of the boy he once was.

He flushed the toilet and washed his hands, because that was the way it had gone on this night. Then he opened the door and saw his best friend, Jimmy Little from grade school (who, despite being the largest of them, they called Little Jimmy). Little Jimmy's large face wrinkled up, he brought a hand up to the area in front of his nose and began to rapidly fan the air.

"Ewwwwwww! Duuuuude!"

The mature adult that Connor was (or tried to be) was immediately embarrassed. He went to apologize to the child in front of him, but when he spoke, what came out was,

"Enjoy!" And then a gleeful cackle as he practically skipped past Little Jimmy on his way down the hallway of his old house. He heard the bathroom door close behind him, but not before Jimmy whispered, "Ewwwwwww!" again.

Connor looked down at his hands. They were as he remembered them being when he was ten years old. He saw none of the hair which had sprouted on the knuckles over the years. The nails weren't yet chewed down to nubs, nor did they contain a never-clearing strip of dark brown grime beneath each of them. Turning them over, he saw that his hands were still soft, not calloused and hardened by years of athletics and hard labor. Not yet scarred by life.

Still feeling like he was inside of a dream, Connor trotted to his childhood bedroom. Prepared himself, for the second time in his life, to experience the wonderful feeling of staying up all night as a child with a group of friends, talking about all of the wonders of the world, thinking that life was nothing but adventures and unending possibilities. That had been their mindset as children. For so long since then that mindset had been lost, trampled by the realities of existence. But now, with the blue droplets in his eyes, Connor was beginning to realize that life could feel just as optimistically wonderful once again.

The boys teased him about his long bathroom break when he entered the bedroom he shared with his brother. Just as he had back then, he made fart noises as he walked through the room until he climbed to the top bunk and settled there. They laughed. He giggled.

Christ, what a feeling it is to giggle again, was what he thought.

They talked.

They had constant conversation with no consequences. Conversation conjured completely from childhood curiosity. The hours flew by. Connor didn't even realize he was tired when he fell asleep later that early morning with a smile on his face, shortly after the sun rose. He drifted off while listening to Little Jimmy talk about why Wolverine would one-hundred-thousand percent kick Batman's ass no problem at all in a no holds barred street fight.

10

Connor was in the bathroom, about to put what were close to the last few drops of the blue liquid into his eyes, when the doorbell rang. He smiled eagerly. The expression was beginning to not feel so foreign to him anymore. Not after the last few days he'd had with the blue substance. And now here was more!

Smiling into the mirror, Connor put the dropper back into the nearly empty vial. He hadn't expected it this quickly, but the first time he had placed the order for the sample vial of MEMLAIN-8, it had shown up overnight, only hours later.

Several hours earlier, before the bell had rung, Connor had ordered a two-month supply of the product after he had woken up and realized how low he was. And how low he felt upon that realization. He had been trying to figure out how he was going to continue to skip out on work (he had never made it for that afternoon shift at the recycling plant) and also afford his MEMLAIN-8 Mental Health Fixer Elixir. Everything LIVAGAIN had promised in the infomercial and all of their other advertisements was true, and he wanted this elixir to continue fixing his mind.

Good times. Good feelings. So much good in one little vial. But how would he pay?

Stressed, he had accessed the website from his phone. Had been scared to find out what insane price this miraculous thing would cost when it wasn't free (he couldn't recall the advertisements ever mentioning a price). After pressing and swiping his way to the payment portion of the webpage, he had been astounded to see:

PAYMENT PLAN APPROVED!
PLEASE CONFIRM QUANTITY TO BE SHIPPED

Submit Quantity: _____

He had only paused for a moment before entering what he hoped would be two months worth of vials to his order. If they had approved of a payment plan, he was sure he would be able to work it out over time.

The last few days had been amazing beyond what Connor could have hoped for. They had been exactly what he needed after the ugliness over River's urn. How could he go back to bad days after the last several had been literally some of the greatest? This was the right thing to do. The responsible and reasonable thing. Whatever bill he would get later would be worth it, he told himself.

Those were his rationalizations as he greedily clicked and clicked and completed the order, relishing the fact that shipping was free all the way from wherever Omnitown was. As an added bonus, the item was to be delivered express.

And here it was, he now thought as he nearly danced from his bathroom, trotting over the broken dishes and the spilled everything that was still on the floor three days after that terrible tantrum. But he didn't mind. Didn't mind that he had been wearing the same clothes and hadn't removed his shoes since he'd had his outburst, or that he had barely eaten anything in those three days. Was unconcerned when it came to crunching over broken glass and grinding it into his carpet. Wasn't bothered by the fact that the pickles he had smashed into the floor were still on the floor, here and there, slowly decomposing. As were other food items from his cabinets and fridge.

He barely noticed any of it – the mess he had made all around him which was really the result of the mess he had made of his life. Barely noticed it because he felt he had no reason to. In a few moments he would take the droplets and be living out a better day. And he wouldn't even have to leave his bedroom to do so.

Connor swiftly made it to the front door, opening it quickly in his eagerness to grab the package from the delivery man and go on with his day (whichever day he chose to go on with once the substance was in his system). But, as the door came fully open, he knew his plans for the day were ruined.

"Kevin," he said atonally as he looked at his brother standing on his doorstep. "Hi."

"Hi? Really? Dude, I've been calling you all day. Why do you do this?"

Kevin made a move to enter the house but Connor blocked him, nearly closing the door on his brother's face. Keeping it open just enough for him to poke his head out, if he felt so inclined. He looked over his shoulder at the mess behind him. A mess that he now very much did notice, along with a smell that suddenly seemed stronger to him as well.

"No. You can't come in right now. The place is a mess," Connor said shakily, his voice a wintry whisper from the space between the door and its frame. Kevin looked at him, perplexed.

"Who are you talking to? I'm your brother. I've peeled you out of puddles of your own puke and piss. You think there's a mess you've made in there that I can't handle seeing?"

"No," Connor said sternly as his brother tried to push the door open. "It was bad on their moving day, Kev. Real bad. I need some time alone."

Kevin took a step back, held his hands up as though a gun were pointed at him. It hurt Connor to see how hurt his brother looked as he reversed from the door.

"I don't think you need any more time alone, Connor. You were already spending plenty of time alone even before you and Becca officially called it quits, and you've been alone since then... Look... I won't come in now because I can tell you're in rough shape and I'm going to respect what you're saying to me. But I need you to do me one favor. Just one."

"I'm already doing you a favor," Connor said coldly. And they both knew he was talking about his promise to stay alive.

"You not killing yourself *isn't a*... You know what? Never mind. I am *very* thankful you're alive. But I want you to actually *live*, know what I mean? In fact, I'm so thankful you're alive that I'm not even going to rag on you about skipping out on the job I got you again," he said, referring to Connor's gig at the recycling plant. "All I'm asking is that you do me this one thing."

Connor fidgeted nervously. He was greatly relieved to not have to apologize again for letting his brother down, this time by not going to work. Any apology would have been a lie, because he finally felt like he *was* living. He wasn't sorry about that whatsoever. The blue elixir. The fixer. He had never felt more alive. Still, he knew he owed his brother.

With a great deal of reluctance, he squeezed the word, "What?" out of his mouth. And saw that Kevin looked visibly relieved to hear it.

"Friday night. Double da—"

"No fucking chance, Kev. I've *told* you about trying to set me up with women."

"I knew you would say that, and I wouldn't be here if it was just *some* woman. But it's not." Kevin grinned obnoxiously as Connor looked at him, nervous about what his brother was set to propose. "You ready for this? You ready? Okay... You ready? Okay... It's Lynsey Merrifield. Lynsey motherfucking *Merrifield.* I *know* you remember her."

Connor did remember her, and though he didn't think of her often these days, she was someone he would never – could never – forget.

She had been his girlfriend for the one magical (and sex-filled) summer before he had mournfully gone off to college, missing Lynsey and that summer until he'd met and moved on with many, many others. Including, eventually, Rebecca. Time and distance, as well as an abundance of young women throwing themselves at him, had undone his relationship with Lynsey more so than anything else. Though for a while he had thought she would be the one. He believed she had felt the same. Somehow it had been nearly twenty years since he had last seen her. And, because he wasn't on social media of any sort, he had no idea how she looked or what she was doing with her life these days.

"Lynsey..." he said, thinking back to so many of their good times that summer. It was enough to bring a small smile to his face. Which was all Kevin needed to see in order to twist his brother's arm further.

"*There* he is! Alright then. I'll tell Lynsey she can join the three of us on Friday night."

"Kevin..."

"Connor. Enough of this, man. I'm practically begging you. And we're talking about Lynsey *fucking* Merrifield here. Do you remember how big her tits are? Do you even remember what a tit feels like?" Kevin asked sincerely.

Connor had to stop himself from smiling again, because, thanks to the blue elixir, he *did* remember what tits felt like again, though he had almost forgotten entirely after not holding one, squeezing one, for over a year. It had been a good few days, he reasoned to himself. He felt better than he had in years. Not to mention that he owed his brother. Owed him a lot.

"Fine. I'd like to find out what tits feel like again," Connor said with a straight face. The two of them laughed like the grown-up children they were for the first time in a long time. When the laughter stopped, Connor could see that Kevin looked like he might shed a tear.

Connor's younger brother turned and walked away quickly, never one to show too much emotion in front of others. As he strode toward his cherry red SUV, he yelled over his shoulder,

"Shave and take a shower, dude. You look and smell like an asshole!"

"I love you too, Kev," Connor said, mostly to himself. Kevin was giving him a one-fingered salute on his way to his car without turning to look back.

Connor shook his head and smiled before closing the door and immediately returning to the bathroom.

11

Connor was back in the bathroom, though he had no intention of showering or shaving as his brother had requested. Not yet. He likely wouldn't do that until Friday, two days from now. Instead, he picked up the vial. Removed the dropper.

Before the doorbell had rung, he had been about to focus on the memory of the first time he had seen the ultrasound of his boy, but now his mind was on a very different track. For one of the few times he could remember in the years since the tragedy had happened, he pushed the thought of his son aside, and welcomed another in.

He thought of a night during that summer before college, when he and his brother had thrown a party shortly after his mother had gone on vacation with their aunt. That was the party where he had met Lynsey, a senior from another high school, a friend of a friend of Kevin's. The friend that Kevin had wound up marrying – his wife, Vanessa, who would be joining Connor, Kevin and Lynsey on their date in two days.

On the night of that party, two decades ago, a group of near-adults had played a children's game: spin the bottle. He remembered his turn, hoping that the bottle would end up pointing at Vanessa of all people, the exotic looking black chick his brother had dared to be seen with in public in their small town. He wanted to witness the look on Kev's face more than anything. But the bottle had landed on Lynsey. And when it had, she'd smiled.

They had kissed, liked the feeling of it. Went on to find a bottle of their own they could consume the contents of. Then they had vanished to his room for hours. Another fun all-nighter from his past.

He continued to think of that night as he applied the blue liquid from the dropper into his eyes. Then he sat cross-legged on the bathroom floor. Connor took the vial, which was now almost empty, and focused as he placed it on the floor in front of him.

Spun it.

Watched it whirl, rotate there, continue twirling for longer than the energy he had provided it with should have allowed. It spun there, twisting, stretching, growing, turning brown. Taffy being pulled, clay being formed. It grew and remoulded until it had gone from a small transparent vial to a much larger brown bottle with its label half peeled off. The floor beneath it had changed as well. Turning from the grungy should-be-white tiles of his bathroom to the concrete ground of the basement of his former home, where the party had been held.

He heard the voices then, just as he looked up and saw them around him.

Connor was no longer in the bathroom at all. Instead, he was back in the unfinished basement that had been a lair to he and his brother throughout their teenage years. He was all at once twenty-one years younger, looking at a younger version of Kevin. Seeing him here through the MEMLAIN-8, Connor realized just how well his younger brother had aged.

Vanessa was there as well, smiling across the circle at Kevin, who was playing it cool and pretending he didn't notice. There were eight of them in that circle, but Connor only looked for one person just then.

Lynsey.

She was blonde, she was beautiful. The first thing Connor did when his eyes set on her was to look at her chest, recalling what his brother had asked him earlier (but twenty-one years later) at the door. No, he hadn't remembered how big her tits were, he realized now.

When he looked up, finally making contact with her eyes, she was smiling at him.

The bottle had stopped, and it was pointing straight at her.

They kissed then, in this reliving of one of the best nights of his life. And, eventually – in the past, and right there in front of his eyes, through a thin blue haze – they found another bottle.

Vanished to his room for hours.

It was four hours later when Connor finally came out of his room, naked and spent, eyes returned from blue to hazel. He was responding to his doorbell again. And this time he knew it wouldn't be his brother on the other side of it when he opened the door.

After momentarily stepping into his bathroom to throw on his robe, he rushed to the front of his house. Opened the door and nearly danced as he saw another brown box, again with no courier in sight. Though this time he hadn't bothered to look for one. It wouldn't have made a difference to him if the package had been dropped from a plane or if it had sprouted legs and walked here itself. It had arrived, and that was all that mattered.

This box was ten times the size of the one the free trial vial had been delivered in. When he picked it up it felt like Christmas. With a laugh, Connor realized that it could be Christmas if he wanted it to be. And, suddenly, that's exactly what he wanted. One particular Christmas.

He thought back to the Christmas in Hawaii. His junior year of college when he had led his football team to the Hawaii Bowl. The gifts that had been arranged for him and his teammates hadn't come in boxes, though they had been unwrapped and were plenty of fun to play with nonetheless. It was a time in his life when he felt like he could simply point at a girl and she would be his, if only for a short duration. It was something he never thought he would again experience in his life. But now he could, and all he had to do was think about it. Remember. Which he would. Maybe twice.

Connor nearly tripped over himself running from the front door directly to his bedroom while ripping open the box containing the MEMLAIN-8.

12

The next two days were bliss. Connor had heard that word previously. Bliss. Though, before those two days, he hadn't truly known what it meant. Not until he went back.

During those two days, Connor had been as happy as he could ever remember. Exploring every pleasant memory he could recall. Going through copies of every family photo he could find – those from his childhood as well as those belonging to the family he had made for himself by adding new branches to the Michaels family tree. This was something he could not have imagined himself being capable of doing previously. Perusing those pictures of his son, wife and daughter, and feeling happiness while doing so. Happiness had refused to be seen anywhere near Connor over the last three years. He was thrilled to reconnect with it now.

He went back.

To being dropped off at summer camp for what may have been the best year of his life until the year he had played spin the bottle with Lynsey. That had been the summer of his first kiss, and his first girlfriend, Ashlynn Gregg, who had been at the girl's camp a few miles down the trail. It had been an epic adventure, those three miles that Connor, Kevin and their friends had broached during what felt like the middle of the night but was only 10:30 PM. It was a mission with the goal of seeing the pretty girls at the camp they had passed while being driven into their campground. The voyage of a few miles between the camps had been worthy of the silver screen to the boys during those days. As had the young romance which emerged from that journey.

He went back.

To prom night, to graduation, to meeting Rebecca in sociology class during their junior year of college, to their wedding, to the birth of their son.

He had hesitated to go back to the day River had entered the world. Thought that reliving it while knowing how things had turned out would shatter him completely. But he was shocked to find that The Pitchman from the commercial had been correct. He could drink in the happy feelings without the hangover of guilt.

He had sat on the edge of his bed at that point, his body in the present while his mind was in the past. He cried happy tears out of now-blue eyes, his hands pantomiming the cradling of a baby boy. He rocked back and forth with the imaginary boy in his arms – River, the boy he could see as though he were real and right there in front of him.

Tears of joy. Again. He would have never believed it could be possible.

Connor was living life on rewind, hitting play for the highlights. Pausing where he wanted to, replaying a certain memory several times in order to relish it thoroughly, more completely than he had the first time around.

He went back.

To attempting and failing to teach River, who had been too young to learn much of anything, how to fish.

To his daughter's birth.

To the last time he and Rebecca had said I love you, before tragedy and grief and blame had consumed that phrase.

He went back.

Revisited a winning touchdown he had thrown during the state championship game during his senior year in high school. There, Connor really absorbed and allowed himself to appreciate what it felt like to be wanted, to be rooted for. Back then he had thought he was loved. By the scouts, the fans, the head coaches from universities all over the country; by the sports networks that televised his games and what was projected to be his rise to the top. But now he knew better. Knew that if you can entertain, if you can offer people something, then adulation begins to feel like affection. Applause begins to feel like adoration.

He revisited both his first home run and the last one.

He even stopped at some point in the past to enjoy a cigarette. Something he hadn't been able to do in the last three years. Now, cigarettes reminded him of death. But with MEMLAIN-8, his vices could be enjoyed without the remorse that was so often attached to them. And Connor made sure to explore those vices thoroughly.

Which is why he went back.

To a life before he had ever thought settling down was a possibility.

A threesome he'd once had.

Returned to college and football, to several big victories. And lived, in real time, in five or ten or (when he had been feeling particularly inspired) twenty minute intervals, all the sex he could remember having after each big win.

This was how he had spent a good chunk of those two days.

Even the times that should have felt bad felt good when he relived them through the blue haze of his eyedrops. He was able to reexperience punching Harold, his ex-wife's current husband, over and over again, right in the mouth. Loving the feeling each time he rewound and replayed that one solid blow he had been able to land on the man who had stolen his family. This time he didn't have to worry about or relive the arrest which had come shortly after. Or the restraining order. Or all the work Kevin had done to smooth things over between everyone involved, for the sake of the child still living. Connor didn't have to worry about the guilt associated with any of that.

He was reliving more than living, enjoying every moment. Hugging people who weren't there, kissing and caressing the air. Making love to his mattress and pillow because it was Lynsey or Rebecca or any number of the girls from high school or college or random nights in bars when he was younger and virile and willing to hump just about anything that moved.

He went back.

Reliving it all again. Savoring every moment.

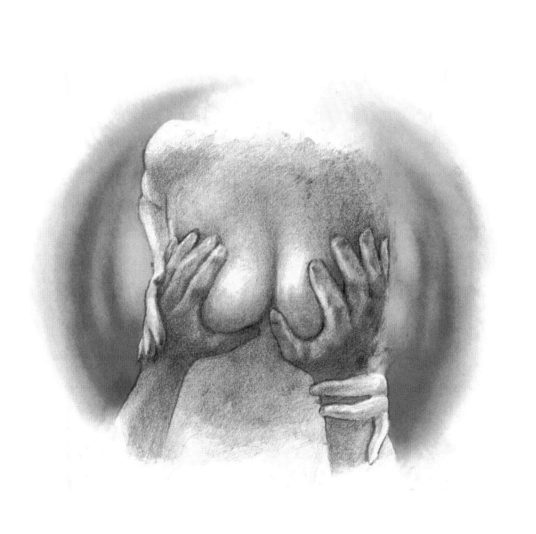

13

It was Friday afternoon in an instant, or so it seemed to Connor. And he was no more shaved or showered than he had been when Kevin had come to his door two days prior and told him to be ready for Friday evening. Though he was now hairier and filthier, Connor was happier. He was not only feeling better, not only somehow less sad, but was genuinely in good spirits. For the first time in years.

It wasn't just that he was no longer sad about his son, he had stopped focusing on the boy obsessively. Or at all. He had barely thought about his son or wife or daughter throughout the last day. And though the memory he was currently visiting was during the years of his marriage, much like when he had lived it the first time, it wasn't his wife he was thinking of. His children had only been an idea then, something he and Rebecca were putting off. Not yet born. This was a time when fatherhood was the furthest thing from his thoughts. This was a time when there were only a few matters on his mind. Constantly. Things he couldn't share with his wife. She likely wouldn't have approved.

Strippers. Hookers.

Not many wives would approve of their young husband cavorting with the likes of those.

During his brief time as a star quarterback on his college team, sex workers had been plentiful. Though, during those years of naivety, when one of the coaches introduced him to what he should have known were escorts, he had simply thought they were huge fans. It was the arrogance of youth as well as an ignorance of how the world worked that had led him to believe that anything positive sent his way was love. Genuine adoration. He had learned the truth quickly during his senior year, when what had made him successful on the playing field seemed to have vanished.

By his senior year, when he was entering his third season as a starter, the coaches of other teams seemed to be aware of his tricks and habits, their teams able to shut him down. The magic he had brought to the game seemingly faded. Without that magic, his own team eventually lost faith, sending him back to the bench while someone else took the reigns of his team. His ascension had lasted only two years. Two sensational seasons, and, just like that, Connor Michaels the rising star had gone supernova and dwindled to darkness all before the world could truly see him shine.

He leaned on Rebecca heavily during those depressing days, which is why they had married nearly straight out of college. It had been the plan all along, though that plan had included Connor making it to the National Football League while Rebecca went to law school to pursue her dream of being a human rights lawyer. The plan had also involved them delaying having children. Putting parenting off until they – particularly Rebecca – were better situated.

They had been able to stick to two-thirds of that plan; Rebecca eventually graduating law school, passing the Bar Exam, and progressing in her career while Connor, after struggling for some time to find steady work, took a job as a quarterback coach for a division three college a town over from where he and his wife had resided. It wasn't what he had expected out of life. Considered it a downgrade. But he put aside the feeling of failure that came with settling for this position long enough to take advantage of the perks that came with it when and how he could. He was part of a team again. And, after a few shaky years, he was a contributor to a winning culture. Which meant big games out of state, and huge road wins. Which meant celebrations.

Strippers. Hookers.

This time he was the one arranging them for the kids who helped get those big wins. But not without taking care of himself and some of his friends on the coaching staff as well. During those days, Connor hadn't realized he had become addicted to sex with nearly every woman who wasn't his wife. Throughout that time, after marriage but before the kids, work as a football coach became less about football and more about comparing one city's strip clubs to the next. The cost of sex in one county in contrast to that in another. The price of pleasure from a person he would never see again. There had been guilt then, about cheating on Rebecca. The guilt had worsened when he continued his bad habits after she had given birth to River, then Cherry. But that guilt hadn't stopped him. Not until his lifestyle had cost him everything.

It was one of those late nights out with the boys, at a club too close to home, that resulted in River's death. And that was when the guilt had become enough to not only end Connor's bad habits, but to nearly end his life the way those habits had ended the life of his son. He hadn't been to a strip club or a sex parlor since. Too much guilt. That was until MEMLAIN-8 took all that guilt away.

On this Friday afternoon, without an ounce of regret, remorse, or recollection of River and the rest of his family, Connor had visited five bordellos in five different cities. Reexperiencing moments of pleasure that the pain of his life had forced him not to dare think about prior to this wonderful elixir putting an end to his bad days.

Thanks to the blissful blue liquid, he couldn't recall being happier. And if he *could* recall a time when he had been happier, all he had to do was think about it until he was there. Soaking it in, collecting joy from the past to bring to the present. Happiness a few drops and a blink away.

He was in the middle of this bliss when he heard his doorbell ring several times in quick succession. This was followed by a banging on the door. Harsh, loud, violent. Like someone was trying to knock the thing down. It was an effort to break himself out of his daze, even more of an effort to dampen his arousal. The serum not only allowed him to access his memories in a remarkable and life changing way, it also seemed to act as an intense aphrodisiac. That side-effect hadn't been listed among the others on the sheet of directions he had received with the elixir, but he certainly didn't mind it. Over the last day, the memories he had been visiting were increasingly those of a more sexual nature, and less of the wholehearted good times he had initially chosen to relive earlier in the week.

The person at the door continued to pound as Connor focused on no longer being aroused. After several difficult seconds, he ran toward the door, navigating his way through the obstacle course of rubbish and wreckage that was now his house.

For the first time in days, he was slightly panicked, distressed, not knowing who it could be or why someone would be beating at his door with such ferocity. Then he remembered the one thing he was supposed to have remembered during the days he had been lost in his remembrances.

His brother.

Kevin, who had probably been trying to reach him on his days-dead cell phone for a long time.

Kevin, who believed he was a suicide risk and was probably worried that Connor was dead inside this home right now. His brother, who had been a defensive tackle in high school, and who would likely knock the door down at any moment.

Two more loud bangs against the door. Then a pause.

"One second! Don't knock the door down! I'm coming, I'm coming!"

He hesitated before opening the door. Had to stop to obtain something from the closet next to the front door first. Connor grabbed the pair of sunglasses he kept on the top shelf of his closet. He had nearly opened the door with his bright blue eyes exposed. It would be hard enough to explain why he had been unreachable for the last couple of days, he didn't want to also have to explain why his eyes were suddenly a different color entirely.

Connor went to the door, looking dishevelled, wearing a bathrobe and shades, smelling like an unkempt farm, and opened it to see that it was indeed Kevin. He was holding something that looked like baggage in his hands. Unlike Connor, Kevin did not appear to be happier than he had seemed two days prior.

"Hey, Ke–"

"Don't 'hey' me right now, Connor. I've called you nearly twenty times since last night. *Twenty* fucking times. I was about to call the cops because... Well, I don't even want to think about that right now." He paused as emotion caused his voice to hitch. Clearing his throat, he went back to being himself. "You still smell like shit. Get shaved. Get showered. Put this on." He shoved what he had been holding into Connor's chest. And held it there until Connor took it.

The item was a garment bag, something Connor hadn't seen since he had placed his suit in one after his son's funeral. He looked at it, expecting the bad memory to make him feel sad. He waited for the recollection of River's funeral to dampen his still heightened mood. But he felt nothing negative. Not even while looking at Kevin's disappointed face. He only smiled slightly at his brother. Kevin did not return the expression.

"I don't know what you're on, but when I get back in three hours, you better be off of whatever it is. Connor, Lynsey is looking forward to seeing you. And so is Vanessa. Try to remember that."

Then he turned and left.

Connor's slight smile remained on his face as he watched his brother walk away from behind his shaded lenses. Yes, he would try to remember that, he thought to himself. He felt unusually optimistic as he considered just what new memories this night might give him access to for the rest of his days.

14

His brother, as usual, had been correct to think ahead on Connor's behalf. The garment bag contained a pair of black slacks along with a purple and white button down long sleeved shirt. At the bottom of the garment bag was a pair of black shoes, a fancy belt, and a pair of flashy multicolored polka dot socks. None of these were clothes that Connor would have picked out for himself, though he couldn't turn them down on this occasion because he had nothing of his own to wear. Since his son's funeral, he had gained over fifty pounds. He still owned most of his old clothes, but the majority of them were far too snug.

After shaving and showering (and using the last bit of MEMLAIN-8 in his system to relive a tryst which had involved a guy's trip to the Dominican Republic, a stranger, and a resort shower), Connor wasn't shocked to find that the clothes his brother had delivered to him fit him pretty much perfectly. Kevin had always had a good eye for that sort of thing.

Connor looked at himself in his bedroom mirror. Smiled at himself in the reflective glass for what seemed to be the thousandth time in the last few days after years of not remembering what his own smiling face looked like. He barely recognized this clean, freshly shaven version of himself. His hair was the only indicator of his recent lack of grooming. It was an awkward length and overdue to be cut, but he was able to use the bit of hair gel he had to fashion it into something presentable that would stay out of his eyes. Eyes he would be using to soak in every detail of this double date. He wasn't so much looking forward to the night as he was looking forward to making new memories.

Exactly at the time Kevin had said he would be there, he was there, banging on the front door. Loud and violent and aggressive. Connor laughed. *I guess Kev decided to just get straight to knocking the door down this time*, he thought before shouting to his brother that he was on his way.

Once he had doublechecked that his eyes were the correct color, he turned to exit his home. But halfway to the front door he had another thought. He remembered something. Something he might need. Just in case.

After going back to his bedroom to grab that certain something, Connor jogged through his house, hurdling and bounding over the mess still all over the floor before opening the door to greet his brother – who looked stunned to see him – with a broad grin and a hug.

"Mom has been asking how you're doing."

"Has she?" was all Connor said to Kevin's statement as Kevin drove the two of them to the restaurant. Connor was freshly shaved and showered for the first time in over a week, and wearing something other than sneakers and jeans for the first time since his son's funeral. Despite the fact that he looked and appeared happier, Kevin knew that Connor wasn't too interested in the date. He assumed that, much like the reason Connor chose to continue living when things were at their worst, he was doing this mostly for Kevin. Still, it was the biggest – the only – step Connor had taken in the right direction in such a long time. Kevin felt he had to try to push him along a bit further.

"I never know what to tell her, Conn. 'He's okay' starts to lose its meaning when you say it and hear it ten thousand times. I think maybe you should tell her yourself. You've got to forgive her at some point."

"Do I?" Connor said. And Kevin braced himself for an onslaught. He hadn't brought this topic up in nearly a year. The last time he had broached the subject, he and Connor had nearly come to blows. It was only after Kevin had apologized profusely to his raging older brother and swore he wouldn't bring the subject of their mother up again that the boiling situation had simmered. Now, as he waited for Connor to lash out and say foul things about the woman who had birthed them both, he nearly regretted asking. It could ruin the night. He had known that before he'd asked. But the fact that there was a night at all to ruin was a sign that maybe his brother was finally waking up from three years of bereavement and self-torture. Kevin had to wonder what of Connor still remained after three years of mournful masochism.

Bringing up their mother was a calculated risk, Kevin understood. But, if this was the only time Connor would actually be open to things, Kevin felt he had to seize the opportunity; lest he risk living with the guilt he would feel from not trying hard enough to reach his brother, the person he knew was beneath the shell of this brother-resembling body beside him in the car. Kevin wouldn't be able to live with himself if he didn't at least attempt to broach the subject and, maybe, eventually, put what was left of his family back together while rescuing Connor from the life he had built for himself. Alone. Married to his misery, sleeping with his sorrows. Becoming less of a human and reminding Kevin more and more of a dog abused by its owner. A violent beast toward everyone who dared to get close. Anyone who tried to help.

Kevin was driving beside what he hoped would be a successful rescue story. An abused dog who was able to come back from the fang-baring distrust every human inspired within him when approached. He was here, he was willing to listen. It meant something even as Connor said nothing. Which was why Kevin continued to try.

"I think you need to call her, Connor. It would do everyone a lot of good. And it would mean some positive progress in your life. That's what this is all about, bro. Baby steps toward anything positive. Isn't that the game plan?"

"You're right." The response was so immediate and surprising that Kevin had to remind himself to keep his eyes on the road. His immediate reaction had been to look at his brother in disbelief. To see if he was being sarcastic. But even before he'd had the time to look, before he could tell Connor to stop kidding, his brother continued. "I've been on some new meds lately, and they've really made me... reflect. I have a lot of good memories with mom. And, looking back, I know she tried. Maybe I'll give her a call tomorrow."

Kevin couldn't have known that Connor was thinking of reliving the phone call he had made to their mother nearly thirty years ago when he had come in first place in his sleepaway camp's shotput competition. That had been an amazing summer, and she had been so proud. He was looking forward... backward... to that phone call.

"Yeah?" was all Kevin could think to say. After that he said nothing else. It was rare to stun him into silence.

"Yeah," Connor parroted noncommittedly as they pulled into the parking lot of Freddy's Alehouse. It wasn't the most lavish of eateries, both brothers knew. It had only recently been updated from dive bar status to legitimate restaurant after extensive renovations and remarketing. They were here for nostalgic reasons, which seemed fitting considering Connor's week. Freddy's had been a place the four who would be on this double date tonight had frequented during that magical summer before Connor had gone off to college. Mainly because it had been lax on checking the identification of older looking teenagers.

Kevin smiled as he looked from the familiar establishment to Connor, still feeling like his older brother's reaction to everything tonight was too good to be true. For the first time in three years, he felt hopeful that things were finally going to be okay. He didn't want to press the issue now, but he would have to make sure to find out just what medication it was that Connor was taking. And to thank whoever had prescribed it.

16

"Do you remember…"

That was how nearly every sentence began during the double date. As he, Lynsey, Kevin and Vanessa sat around a table loaded with drinks and appetizers – the two women sitting across from the two men – each person other than Connor seemed to want to do nothing other than reminisce. This was why Connor hadn't often wanted to leave his home or spend time with people from his past. It was mostly because they were still there. In the past. Stuck there, as if incapable of moving on from their better days. Reminding him of how bad his days had gotten.

Typically, the looking back depressed him, caused him to think of how far his life had fallen. Now he simply felt bored by it, knowing that these half-remembered retellings of times long past couldn't compare to his going back and reliving them as they happened. If the entire night out would be about recounting memories that he could relive on his own, for real, then he was starting to feel like leaving his home might have been a mistake.

The last memory testing question had been asked by Lynsey. It was about a weekend a group of them had spent at a friend's beach house just before Connor had gone off to college. A wild party. Lots of booze, drugs, the police being called. Sex. It was a time when life was fun, and the future seemed like a place full of eternal hope.

Yes, he remembered. He had been there two afternoons ago. Which is why he didn't truly care to hear this half-hearted rendition of that weekend. Even if Lynsey did remember more than she was describing for them tonight, Connor knew there was a level of debauchery which had occurred at the beach house that Lynsey would never admit to Vanessa and Kevin.

Connor did his best to play along. To listen to each of them tell their part of the story of that weekend. Added the parts he was supposed to add. Described his perspective of events as the others described their own, as though he didn't remember them in crystal clear detail. He listened to the false-sounding laughter that was the response. Retorted with false laughter of his own when appropriate.

"Do you remember..."

This time it was Vanessa. She asked about the party the boys had thrown way back when. The party when the group had all been together for the first time. Spin the bottle. Connor had been there thrice since receiving the cloudy blue serum.

It was then Connor realized that something was irritating him about these stories; it wasn't only boredom and the fact that they didn't compare to going back and experiencing the real thing in real time. As the night progressed, Connor understood what was bothering him: for the first time since receiving the MEMLAIN-8, he felt betrayed by his special blue eyedrops.

And it was because of Lynsey. Because of how she looked.

He knew it wasn't fair to Lynsey; time diminished and defeated all. But each time he glanced her way, he couldn't help but think about how beautiful this same woman had been in the reliving of his memories that week. If he hadn't just seen so clearly what she had once been, this change in her appearance wouldn't have seemed so jarring.

As Connor looked across the table at her, he couldn't help but think that it made sense to him why Lynsey was willing to go out with a reputed loser such as he. If she was the way she looked, then she was desperate. Either that, or she likely hadn't heard how much of a loser Connor was. Or, she had heard how much of a loser he was, and had been convinced by Kevin and Vanessa that the rumors of his losing ways were overstated. But how could anyone not immediately know the man to be a loser? His life involved a dead child and a broken family. He was once a former college football star. A star that had never fully risen. Now he was known to be a drunken, odd-jobbing, failure of a man. A failure of a father. Connor had to wonder what it said about her that she would even agree to sit across from him.

From what Kevin had told Connor in the car before they had begun to speak about their mother, Lynsey had been through the birth of two children and the death of a marriage. A recently labelled divorcee, she still wore the years of bad matrimony on her skin like the very makeup she used to cover her blemishes. To mask her wrinkles. Her laugh lines. The passing of time itself.

She was another reminder to him of how nothing was as good as it used to be. A reminder that living – that being alive – is an illusion, or at the least a contradiction. Because to live is to decay. To be alive is to rot slowly, to barely notice it, only to be surprised by the inevitable result of the signs that had been there the entire time. Decades of deterioration from delivery 'til death.

Inevitable decay, that was what Connor was thinking about as he looked at Lynsey's breasts. He remembered them being much higher. Fuller. Better then. Now they seemed to almost be blending in with a soft and protruding middle, turning what was once a figure 8 of a body into what was more or less a shapeless mass.

Lynsey caught him looking at her chest. Connor looked away. Down. Noticed his own chest. Wondered when his pecks had become a bosom, and when that bosom had become nearly as big as Lynsey's. His own gut was far more keg than the six-pack it had once been, though it had taken many a six-pack of beer to get it this way. He couldn't even use childbirth as an excuse.

He was a man sitting across from a woman. A woman who had been a girl once attracted to the boy he used to be. The jock. The hard bodied stud. The star of the football team. Now, here he was, a bottle of beer and a glass of whiskey in front of him, he and his brother sharing a turbo nacho cheese plate, his once well muscled body sloppy and toneless, his hairline rapidly running backward and away from a face that had previously been smooth skinned with a square jawline. Cigarettes and booze had left that skin blemished, prematurely wrinkled and loose. Somewhere along the line, his square jaw had begun to turn to sagging jowls as he had developed a secondary and possibly the beginnings of a tertiary chin.

"Do you remember..."

Music continued to play softly in the background, conversations from the other diners in the bar floated in bits and pieces toward their table. There were a few lingering glances from the patrons toward Vanessa, whose brown skin always stood out wherever they went in this town. As always, the group pretended they didn't notice. The other three sitting with Connor were all smiles and laughs, happily reunited. He did his best to fake it, to match their energy. But how could they be truly happy seeing what the world was like? What Lynsey and Connor had become?

How could they be happy being forced to sit here with a loser like him?

That's what was on Connor's mind during all of the reminiscing.

He was in the middle of feeling as though Lynsey could not possibly want anything to do with this version of him when he felt a foot against his foot. Then a foot against his ankle. His calf. Rising. His knee. Eventually, the foot was running along his thigh. Higher...

He looked down at the foot, then at its owner across from him. Lynsey, smiling demurely at him. Winking in a way that was barely a wink. Lynsey, perhaps mistaking his evaluation of the position of her breasts relative to the progression of time as an indication that he was still interested in her. She was making it clear, with her very dexterous toes under the table, that she was interested in him. Even with his thickening face and bloated belly, and her sagging breasts and loosening skin, she still wanted to take these versions of their life-worn bodies down an old road. Back to the days when she had used terms like "Gone all the way", and he had used terms like "She let me bone" when they described to their respective friends the special development that had happened during their long-ago relationship. He wondered how she would describe sex with him at this age to her friend beside her. Would she keep it a secret that they had gone all the way? Would he still want to brag that she had let him bone?

He looked at her, forced a smile. The entire while he was editing her. Using the very clear image of the younger her in his mind as a reference point. He was trying to airbrush the face of the version of her in front of him. Trying to whittle away the excess weight around her middle, attempting to imagine what those thick thighs would look like if only they were toned.

What he realized, as he took in all of her flaws, was that he didn't have to try so hard to imagine her as she used to be. Why waste the mental energy when he could experience it for himself?

"Do you remember..." Kevin began.

Connor did remember. But he also remembered that, right now, he would rather be elsewhere. Desperately.

Without any warning to the others in his company, Connor swallowed the last of his whiskey, rose, and excused himself from the table.

17

"Are you sure he's okay?" Lynsey asked Kevin.

Kevin and Vanessa exchanged a brief look he hoped Lynsey didn't notice. What could he say to that question? Was Connor okay? The simple answer was no. He had hoped his brother would be okay tonight, but the way he had gotten up from the table and walked off without any warning or reason concerned Kevin. The fact that it had been over five minutes and he hadn't returned was even more troubling.

"He..." Kevin started, stammered, and was relieved to find that his wife continued on where he would have bumbled along, making clumsy excuses for his brother. He was smooth, a natural salesman, but when it came to talking about Connor, Kevin always seemed to fumble. It was a minor miracle that Lynsey was even here at all. Most of that had been thanks to Vanessa, who was currently in the middle of saying,

"...his first date since his son's death. And he's been dealing with some anxiety issues. Just give him a few minutes to shake it off and get loose. It's not every day that a guy is rocked by a stunner of a blast from the past like you, Lyns." Not for the first time during the last week, Kevin considered his wife to be a blessing. Lynsey seemed to accept the explanation. They continued to have half-hearted conversation as they waited. As they worried.

After five more minutes had passed, Kevin texted and called Connor. Received no response to either. That's when the conversation at the table became stagnant. Awkward.

Ten minutes later, the situation became truly uncomfortable. And when Kevin went to check the men's bathroom and didn't find his brother there, he became legitimately concerned. A quick search outside of the restaurant only added to his worries.

"He's not in the bathroom," Kevin said when he returned to the table, his face red with embarrassment. "He's not outside or in my car either. And he's not answering his phone. I'm really sorry Lynsey. Really, *really* sorry. He's going through a rough time and I thought this might help him out of it. I was wrong. I'll take care of your bill and your ride home."

Lynsey looked at him from across the table and smiled sadly. She, too, had had years full of many bad days. And it seemed like this was just another one of those.

"It's fine," Lynsey said, and meant it. "Funny how life turns out, huh? Who would have thought so many of us would just be trying to pick up the pieces? I definitely understand." For a moment Kevin thought that she might cry. Lynsey excused herself to go to the bathroom.

Vanessa and Kevin both watched her walk away before she was covered up by a small group of women heading to the bathroom behind her. Once she was out of sight, Kevin said,

"What a Goddamn clusterfuck. I want to say 'I'm gonna kill him', but this is my fault. What did I think was gonna happen? Connor is a wreck. I gave him two days notice and he still hadn't even showered by this afternoon. I just... Fuck. I just... I just want my big brother back."

Vanessa leaned across the table and took her husband's large hands into her own as she watched his shoulders slump and his head sag until his forehead nearly touched the table. She hadn't seen him look so defeated since the last time Connor had gotten himself into serious trouble with the law. When he had punched his ex-wife's new husband in the face. All because the new man in Rebecca's life had suggested to Connor that his daughter might be a bit slow for her age. Perhaps due to the emotional trauma she had undergone after surviving what had killed her brother.

That had been a bad day. And things had only gotten worse.

With the way Connor had been constantly spiraling without any sign of improvement, Vanessa couldn't imagine things getting any better. But she had to be positive. And she knew she would have to lie to her husband for the sake of sharing that positivity. Vanessa was going to tell Kevin that things would improve for his brother. It was one of the very few lies she ever told him. She raised one of her husband's hands to her lips, gave it a kiss. Said,

"This is still a huge step he took today, Kevin. Things are going to get bett—"

A shriek disrupted the ambiance of the establishment.

The music still played, but most of the conversations had stopped. Kevin's head snapped up at the sound of the scream. He and Vanessa locked eyes, both of them knowing immediately that this could not be good.

Another shriek. Then another.

"Oh my God!"

"Someone call the police!"

An additional shrill squeal. Screeches and shouts.

Then, from one of the employees:

"Please, everybody settle down! No need to panic!" The employee, a young waitress, sounded very panicked.

"There's a bit of a situation in the lady's bathroom! But we'll have it under control soon!"

Another shriek rang out, immediately contradicting what the shaky but brave young woman had just said. Then, further making her a liar, came the sound of running bodies.

Both Vanessa and Kevin turned toward the direction all the commotion was coming from. They were looking toward the bathrooms, where Kevin had previously gone to search for his brother... in the men's room.

"No..." Kevin moaned, his voice low and unstable with his not wanting to believe what he was seeing.

Lynsey was racing from the bathroom area. Sprinting – her hair and breasts bounding up and down, her face red and tight with concern – all the way to the table. She nearly bowled everyone over when she got there, gripping the table as though she had just chased it down for fear it was about to run away. Face flushed, white knuckled, short of breath, Lynsey shakily said,

"Your brother... Guys, Connor is out of it. And he's... It's bad, guys. They're going to arrest him if you can't get him out of here *right* now."

"Fuck." Kevin had uttered the profanity and bolted before Lynsey had finished her statement.

Vanessa stood, both she and Lynsey watching Kevin as he ran in the direction that people were either beginning to mill around or run away from. They watched him shoulder his way through the crowd and into the bathroom area. Vanessa was full of dread as she wondered what new piece of bad news her husband was running toward.

Knowing she would have to find out one way or another, Vanessa took a deep breath and quickly followed Kevin to the women's bathroom.

18

Connor wanted Lynsey. Had wanted her even as he sat across from her. But had not wanted the version of her he had been sitting across from. Partway through the conversation, he realized that he didn't have to settle for that version of her. Or for this version of himself, for that matter.

After excusing himself from the table, he had gone to the men's room, remembering the item he had returned to his bedroom to get before departing his house for this failure of a double date.

Once inside the bathroom, and once it was clear of others, he had looked into the mirror after putting a drop of MEMLAIN-8 into each eye.

Just a small amount. A quick fix.

He wanted Lynsey. He wanted things to feel like they had back then, when they were better. Before life, full of its bad days, had ruined them. Worn them down. Back when they weren't becoming wrinkled and saggy and getting heavier each day. He wanted the Lynsey who wouldn't be anticipating the sob story of how his son had accidentally died. He wanted the summer where a girl like Lynsey would have scoffed at the stretchmarks and spanx that were her life now. He wanted the girl who wouldn't have looked twice at an aging overweight loser like him.

What Connor truly wanted was the simplicity of what was. Even if only for ten minutes. Just a little break from the right now. A quick fix from the depression that was this evening.

When his eyes had turned blue, Connor went into the stall and remembered a day which had occurred two decades earlier, when he and Lynsey had ducked into a bar just like this one, but with absolutely no intention of sitting and drinking.

19

"Sir! You shouldn't go in there!" someone cried out, but Kevin was already past that person and into the place he had been told he shouldn't have gone into.

Vanessa wasn't far behind him, and Lynsey was there too. After some hesitation, she had decided that Kevin and Vanessa would need all of the help and support they could get. Especially since the screaming and commotion hadn't stopped, and the police were now likely on their way.

The two women watched Kevin storm into the women's room just as someone told him not to enter. That same someone – a skinny busboy who looked like he was in way over his head – put his quivering hand up toward them, palm out, indicating that they stop.

For a moment they did. Until they heard Kevin's shouting voice adding to the chaos in the restaurant.

20

About ten minutes before Kevin burst into the women's bathroom and shouted, Connor had been in the bathroom stall of the men's room. This was prior to the shrieking and the commotion in the restaurant.

He had been on the toilet seat, tongue kissing the air in front of him, his hands pawing at it, grabbing blissful chunks of nothing. Relishing every bit of it because what he was seeing and feeling was Lynsey, young and taut and burden-free.

He had remembered this day only when her foot – the foot of the real her who was now sitting awkwardly at their table wondering where he had gone – had run its way up his leg.

They had loved to fuck in random places. And the bathroom of a bar had been one of those places during that thrilling adventure of a summer.

With that memory in mind, he had taken the elixir and had decided to relive that tryst in real time.

In his memory, it had been a quick fling in a stall. What he had forgotten, unsurprisingly, considering they had both been spectacularly drunk that day, was that she had insisted they go from the men's bathroom into the women's at some point during their tryst. Telling him that no one would interrupt them there. Reminding him that the baseball game playing in the bar had been about to end, and the bathroom they were currently in would be flooded with men in minutes.

They had paused only to compose themselves enough to sneak to the women's room, a place which was vacant nearly all the time in a bar like the one from that summer. Connor had wondered why they hadn't started out there in the first place.

He had waited for her to leave the bathroom first. Then, walking halfway hunched over, eighteen-year-old Connor had scurried out of the men's room and into the women's bathroom after her.

He had done that twenty-one years prior.

He did the same on this night, in this bar, just a minute before Kevin had initially entered the men's room to look for him. And not long before that initial shriek had announced the official destruction of their night.

When Connor had stumbled into the women's bathroom fondling the air, grasping it, romancing it with passion, a bulge straining against his pants for everyone who might be in the bathroom to see, he was fortunate that no one was in the bathroom to see it.

In his mind, he and the young Lynsey were now entering one of the stalls on that long-ago day during their tryst in the bar.

In reality, he had made his way alone into one of the stalls. Had finally sat down. Releasing a sigh of relief, he lowered the pants and boxers that had been so constraining him.

In his mind, after minutes of intense and passionate making out with the young Lynsey, he had entered her.

In reality, the present version of Lynsey had entered this bathroom.

A few other women had trailed in after her, making small talk, chatting. That chatter had stopped when they thought they heard something from one of the stalls.

Panting. Grunting. Several moans.

The three women who had entered the bathroom after Lynsey had looked at her. She had looked at the three of them, and they had all exchanged the same uneasy expression. Most of them smiled nervously, wondering if they were hearing what they thought they were hearing.

Someone grunting... seeming to be straining. It was almost funny, until there was a violent banging on the door from inside of the stall.

Lynsey looked at the women. They all looked at the stall just in time to see it burst open.

Then had come the shriek, the screaming, followed by Lynsey's sprint out of the bathroom away from what she had just seen.

21

Now, Kevin entered that same women's bathroom, minutes after that initial shriek. Vanessa and Lynsey were not far behind him.

He crashed though the door, bracing himself to see his bigger brother perhaps hurting himself, maybe having one of his tantrums and damaging the property. Another charge that Kevin would have to spend several thousand dollars in legal fees on in order to keep his brother out of prison.

Kevin had bounded into the bathroom, readying himself to face off against the raging bull that was his brother. But when he saw what he saw, it shattered his heart, and he didn't know what to do. Didn't know what to do other than to add to the commotion in the restaurant.

Kevin Michaels looked at his older brother in the middle of the women's bathroom, and let loose a mournful cry.

22

In Connor's reliving of that tryst with Lynsey those two decades prior, he and the girl with the amazing rack and sex drive like a jackrabbit had been inside of the stall. She had been on top of him, riding. But he had felt inspired that day. Strong. Had wanted to show her how much of a man he was.

After lifting her up in the deserted bathroom of that dingy bar, her legs still astride his hips, he had pressed her back against the door, given her three hard thrusts, and then the door had burst open.

Over twenty years ago, a young Connor and Lynsey had crashed out of the bathroom stall and onto the floor. Giggling, trying not to roar with laughter at the ludicrousness of the situation. All those years ago, they had rolled on that dirty bathroom floor, partially naked and laughing. When Lynsey had gone to stand up, Connor had pulled her back down. Said,

"You did say that no one ever comes in here, right?"

And then he had taken her right there in the middle of the women's room, on the ground, pumping into her violently. Trying to hurry it up while enjoying every moment. Squeezing at her soft parts. Savoring every stroke.

It had been one of the wildest days of his life.

Until two decades later...

23

What Kevin saw when he ran into the bathroom was his brother on the floor. All over the floor, actually. His pants were around his ankles, his ass was exposed. He was kissing the ground, humping it too. Connor was grinding himself into the tiles like the floor was a woman. A lover. Crashing down into it in a way that Kevin couldn't understand. But what really concerned Kevin, what had made him cry out, was the blood. The blood that had begun to pool from beneath Connor's mouth where he was kissing the ground with a violent passion that no man should have toward a walked-upon surface.

Kevin shouted as Connor continued humping the ground, leaking from the mouth where his teeth were sawing into the backs of his lips, the filthy tiles accepting his embrace with cold, unmoving solidity.

Kevin went to the floor beside his brother, wrapped his arms around Connor's naked waist. Cringed as he felt his brother's hardness against his forearm.

Kevin had gotten Connor to his feet when the door opened. Vanessa and Lynsey entered.

Both of them added to the noise of the restaurant.

It was too much for Vanessa, seeing her brother-in-law's rigid and now badly discolored and awkwardly bent penis exposed to the air as he seemed to be chewing at nothing at all, blood smeared all over his face and running down his chin. Kevin's wife turned and left the bathroom, leaving her husband to attend to his half naked brother who was thrashing in his arms.

Lynsey decided to do the opposite. She approached the two men in hopes of helping Kevin settle Connor down, until, for a moment, she was stunned into standing still. Kevin couldn't see Connor's face from his position restraining him from behind, but Lynsey could. And it was an image that would haunt her memories for the remainder of her days.

Connor was gone. Not there at all. Elsewhere.

He was kissing and gnawing at the air. Licking, sucking, even as blood bubbled up from his ruined mouth, causing a red goatee to form around his lips and chin.

Connor was in another location even as he stood there staring with unblinking eyes in front of him. At Lynsey. Through Lynsey.

Then he said her name.

"Oh, Lyns!" was sent out on a moan. But his voice was different. Younger. There was a strange innocence to it, an oddness that chilled the air. Both Kevin and Lynsey felt it. Looked at each other. Froze. Until he spoke again.

"Lynsey, God fucking damn you, you're so good," he moaned in a boyish voice. And Lynsey watched as the distraught and vacant man continued thrusting his groin at the air in front of him. He let out a loud lustful exhale. He cried, "Lynsey!" and then erupted right then and there, just as the door behind Lynsey erupted as well.

Semen out of Connor.

Policemen entering the bathroom.

The last thing Lynsey noticed about Connor, before Kevin was ripped away from him and he was restrained by the two officers who had entered the room, was his eyes.

She would think about this moment for decades, and always convince herself that it was a combination of stress and poor lighting that had caused it. But she could have sworn that the man's eyes had been blue for a moment. Bright blue. Then, when the police had wrenched his arms behind his back while covering his lower half with a towel, Connor had blinked, still staring in Lynsey's direction. And she had seen the color of his eyes fade. Change. Had watched them revert from blue to hazel.

Stress and the lights, she would tell herself for the rest of her time in this world. Stress and the lights.

Except that stress and the lights didn't account for what happened after Connor had finally blinked. After he had stopped looking through Lynsey and actually registered her. And couldn't understand why she had changed so drastically.

She saw this in his eyes as well – this confusion – and would never ever doubt what she saw next. Lynsey witnessed her old friend and ex-lover's mind fracture in that moment. A blue blink, a blank stare. Realization. Confusion. Then the breaking.

The rest of the commotion in the restaurant was silenced as Connor loosed a howl that caused everyone in the entire building to stop. To not know what to do.

One of the officers attempting to restrain Connor figured out what to do rather quickly. Concerned about the wellbeing of his hearing, and generally tired of the situation entirely, he removed his taser from his belt, pressed it against Connor's stomach. And brought the building to complete silence.

24

The cigarette smoke burned his eyes, made his mouth dry and taste like a firepit. But he was nearly through his third one that hour, and would no doubt light a fourth as soon as this one was done.

Kevin only smoked when he was extremely stressed. Both he and Connor had vowed to quit shortly after River had died. But the last week had been among the most stressful in his life; a life that had already seen him lose a father and a nephew, both suddenly and prematurely. He hadn't been prepared for either of those departures, had hoped for more time. Now, as he was in the process of feeling as though he was losing his brother, he realized that a quick end might be the merciful thing in certain situations. It was a thought he hated to give credence to, but it was one which wouldn't leave his mind.

Kevin was currently walking toward his car in the parking lot outside of the hospital his heavily medicated brother was temporarily calling home. This was a week after Connor had been arrested and eventually taken to the mental health floor of this facility.

After seeing the state his older brother was in, Kevin couldn't help but wonder if Connor wasn't just playing out some slow and painful ending. One that probably felt never-ending to the former football star and family man, now just another patient in the mental ward. A number on a file.

Connor had received a diagnosis not long after being admitted to the hospital: Schizophreniform Disorder; potentially Schizophrenia if his symptoms didn't improve after some more time in observation and on medication. The 'S' word. He had suspected that Connor might be mentally ill for some time now. Anxiety and depression were certainly understandable. Any number of mood disorders would explain a lot. Though this was the diagnosis that no one wanted.

How do you help someone who doesn't know what's real from what's imaginary?

Kevin was about to light his fourth cigarette of the last hour when his phone rang. He answered it, thankful to speak to someone about all he had been thinking.

"Hey, Ness. I hope your day's going better than mine," Kevin said to his wife.

"No change?" Vanessa asked him.

"He won't stop talking about those fucking eyedrops. And no one can make heads or tails of it."

There was silence on the line, but it was a comfortable silence. An accepting silence. They had talked about all of this before. Connor's obsession with the eyedrops. The way he kept insisting that he didn't have to deal with his issues anymore if they would just let him get his eyedrops. A fixer elixir, he had said. An instant cure for mental illness. Then he had spewed all manner of profanities and curses and wishes of violence upon the hospital staff for not knowing what they were doing or how to help anyone.

'LIVAGAIN! In Omnitown!' he had shouted repeatedly, telling them constantly about this miracle company from an unknown town, insisting for them to get the brown box in his room full of vials of a blue substance he called MEMLAIN-8.

But all of it was nonsense, non-existent, according to searches of both Google and Connor's home.

Connor's bungalow had nearly caused Kevin to empty the contents of his stomach upon entering. Because the contents of Connor's entire kitchen had been thrown all over the house. Dishes and drinking glasses were shattered and scattered everywhere he looked. Kevin saw an exploded jar of mayonnaise, the majority of the mayo once inside of it was now a thick, yellowed series of splotches dried and hardened against the kitchen wall. Pickles were all over the floor from the kitchen to the living room. A bag of rice had been emptied and sprayed about the place like confetti. Chips. Crackers. Popcorn seeds from torn open bags. Among it all, there were ants in hordes, and the occasional mouse or two taking their share of the buffet Connor had provided them. The mice seemed to be finding their way into the living area from the several holes which made up most of one of Connor's walls. Holes Kevin could clearly visualize his older brother making with his fists.

If he'd had any idea how bad it had been going for Connor, Kevin would have driven him straight to the hospital last Friday night rather than subjecting him to a date he clearly hadn't been ready for. Now, a week later, he would have to practically break his brother out if he wished to see him anywhere but the hospital. They were fortunate about that, in a sense. Lucky that it was a hospital he was locked inside of and not a jailhouse. The police could very well have thrown him in a cell instead of taking him to the mental ward. The officers had taken pity on him, one of them a fan of Connor's from his college football days.

"What's next?" Vanessa asked softly.

"Nothing's really next. He stays. There's nowhere for him to go. You saw the way his house was. Christ, I'm not sure if he can ever live on his own again. He can't stay with us because of the kids. He has no friends. He cut all ties with his old coworkers and teammates when he quit coaching. He hasn't been rational to anyone for a while; I mean, he hasn't even talked to our mom in years simply because she was the first one brave enough to tell him to deal with his role in River's death and take accountability. And now he won't let go of this magical eyedrop bullshit. Where else can he go? Plus, there's the fact that he doesn't even know that Rebecca found out what happened and doesn't want him having anything to do with Cherry. You know what that will do to him, Ness? I want to be mad at her, but I can't even blame her... If he wasn't my brother..."

"Yeah, but he *is* your brother. And he's been your best friend your entire life. It doesn't look good now, Kevin, but we have *time*. Like you said, he's not going anywhere, he's being taken care of. Give it time. I know that's hard to hear, but as long as we have time Connor will always have a chance."

"Yeah. Let's hope you're right," Kevin said, and felt slightly comforted by the words he didn't quite believe but appreciated nonetheless. They exchanged I love yous. Kevin finished cigarette four. Then lit and finished cigarette five for good measure before hopping in his car. He rolled the windows down in hopes of airing out his clothes before getting home to his family.

Time. Kevin reflected on the word as he headed for home, wondering all the while just what new piece of cruelty time would have in store for all of them next.

25

Connor wasn't in a good way. He was sedated but he was still seething. No matter what they gave him, it didn't chase the madness away.

He was mainly angry because he didn't have to be here even if he had to physically be here. He wasn't saying that he should be let out. He wasn't saying that he didn't deserve to be in a hospital, medicated. He didn't care what they decided to do with him. All he wanted was his fucking eyedrops, and no one was willing to bring them to him. Not even his ingrate of a little brother, who had lied to Connor's face when telling him that he had searched for the box full of MEMLAIN-8 and hadn't found it. It was a huge brown box and was in the middle of his bedroom. It wouldn't be hard to find, Connor knew. He wondered what his brother's motives truly were.

Kevin had probably tried the stuff and was now hoarding it for himself while letting his brother suffer. Connor was starting to consider this to be a possibility. The more Connor thought about it, the more he believed that the entire date night had been a setup. To get him out of the house and then send him here so they could take his shit, rob him of the little he had left. It was all a ruse. Kevin and Vanessa were probably sitting somewhere, blue-eyed, reliving the best of times while Connor was here, drugged up and wallowing.

The thought of it made him incensed. Made his adrenaline flow, his pulse rate rise. There were a thousand pleasant memories he could be reliving right now. Instead, he was in a hospital room with his head fuzzy, his coherent thoughts fleeting, not able to reliably remember much of anything. Except for the fact that his brother had put him here.

Connor began to get out of bed, was set to enter the hallway and rage at anyone who wouldn't tell him the truth about what was going on. But just as he had shouted his first stream of guttural profanity, the door swung open. And Connor nearly wept.

In front of him was the answer to all of his problems. He had never felt so relieved in his life as he did when he heard what the person who had opened the door had to say.

"Hello, Connor," said the owner of the up-tempo voice that was somehow a calming touch. A gentle breeze. The owner of that voice patted his red blazer, indicating his breast pocket, inside of which was a black Timepiece full of bright blue sand. The Pitchman continued,

"Has it turned out that the present isn't the gift you expected it to be? Future not looking too bright? How about a little time off? A break, a trip down memory lane. A vacation to the good times. You see, I do believe I have what you need right here for you..."

Connor was surprised to see that no one made a fuss when he and The Pitchman left his room. They walked down several flights of steps and all the way to the exit without anyone saying a word, including The Pitchman. He only walked, leading Connor even though they trekked side-by-side.

The only thing odder than the lack of reaction to Connor roaming freely in the hospital hallways was The Pitchman's hat. Connor couldn't stop looking at it. By the time they got to the exit and approached the automatic doors that would lead Connor to freedom, he felt as though he absolutely had to say something about The Pitchman's fedora.

"Your hat," Connor stammered out. And suddenly the air around them became hot, hazy. The air around them felt as though it had grown thick. So thick that the remainder of his words seemed to have issues making their way through to his companion, travelling from Connor's mouth sluggishly. He felt as though he were speaking in slow motion. "Can't you feel it? Your hat is burning."

The Pitchman looked at him with brilliant blue eyes gleaming from behind his red-rimmed glasses as the automatic doors opened for them. He blinked as if realizing Connor was there for the first time. Turned his eyes slowly upward as if to see what Connor was referring to.

That was as close to a response as Connor would get. Because the man wearing the fedora with the flaming feather raging from the side of it only looked at Connor indifferently before proceeding forward. Once they had stepped through the doors of the hospital, The Pitchman said,

"Could I interest you in a trip down Memory Lane..."

And the two continued to walk into the bright and shining day.

26

That would have been a nice way to end things for Connor. A pleasant stroll toward Memory Lane on a bright and sunny day. In a sense, it *was* the way things ended for Connor. It was how it had played out in his mind, anyway. It was what he had been seeing as things truly unfolded.

In his mind, he had walked out of his room with The Pitchman. In reality, he had actually sprung out of bed when a nurse had come to take him for his daily exercises and activities. He had bowled over and knocked the nurse unconscious. He did the same to a second nurse. Then another. And then to whoever stepped in his way next. He was no longer a quarterback, but now a lineman, a running back, a bowling ball rolling straight through a row of pins.

Connor Michaels was a raging bull, and all the world was red. He had rumbled his nearly three-hundred-pound frame through the hallways, making anyone who had signed their name to his chart regret not suggesting he be put on a stronger dose of sedative, or restrained outright.

He had been nonviolent. That would be the argument they would make. That would be what the staff would tell their superiors and the board that oversaw hospital regulations. That's what they would eventually tell Kevin, and Connor's mother.

"He was listed as a nonviolent patient. How were we to know?"

Perhaps they couldn't have known. But ignorance wouldn't let them off the hook. There would be no acceptable explanation to justify a hospital allowing a suicide risk, a man of that size, to flee from the mental health ward. Get out. Escape.

Run to the roof.

27

A few minutes after Kevin had pulled out of the far-too-expensive hospital parking lot, while he was on his way home to be with his wife and kids, his brother was plummeting from the roof of the same hospital that Kevin was driving away from.

They would find him there. Connor. A red splotch atop a car in the hospital parking lot. Fallen there, crashed there. Dead. There.

A mess of a man late in his life, and now more mess than man in his death.

Kevin was devastated when he found out, receiving the bad news after answering his phone while he drove. As he made the U-turn back to the hospital after getting off the phone with one of its representatives, all he could think of was that Connor had lied to him.

Even though Kevin had found a way to forgive him for everything he had done over the years, Connor had finally, truly, let him down for good. Because Connor had gone back on his word. And had decided that the last act of his life would be to break the promise he had made to his little brother.

Post-Mortem

Memory Lane.

North. East. South. West. It was all one Endless Route.

Connor didn't like the walk down Memory Lane this time as much as he had the first. In fact, he didn't like it at all. Mostly because it was so hot.

So hot because every house on Memory Lane was on fire.

Every house was the same house once again. Though, this time, they were each the single storey home he did his best not to think of. Inside of each of these exact same houses – the curtains now ash, the windows exploded from the rise in temperature – he saw a scene. Inside of every single house, he saw the same moment of his life.

It was the moment he had lit the cigarette after sitting down in his recliner following a late night out of drinking and doing things he would never tell his wife about. With people she could never be introduced to.

He had lit that cigarette at close to three in the morning, despite the fact that his wife always bothered him about smoking inside of the house. Had previously begged him not to do so. But he simply wanted to relax, have a final beer before bed, and watch a bit of television while enjoying the night's last cigarette. Was that too much to ask? He certainly hadn't thought so then.

Now, Connor stood there on Memory Lane, looking into every house for something different, seeing it was all the same. Witnessing himself passing out in the living room.

Watching that cigarette fall from his hand. Hit the rug. Watching the rug catch fire. And witnessing that fire spread freakishly fast along the carpet to the rooms behind the passed-out Connor before it began to consume the room he was in.

Connor observed from outside as his little girl rushed into the scene, her pajamas and little head on fire. She had woken up in time to run out of the room she shared with her brother (who she had tried to wake, but who slept like a stone) and into the living room where the fire was raging. She had screamed,

"Daddy!"

She had screamed,

"Wake up!"

Then she had simply screamed.

By some miracle he had woken up. *Some* miracle – portions of one but not enough. Not the true miracle he had needed that early morning. Because, while his daughter had made it to him, hair on fire in every sense. While he had held her, smothered the flames from her head and deadened the burning, he had heard his son begin to cry out.

And then his wife a moment later.

A family of four. Several decisions to be made.

Connor had made the simplest one, which was to carry his daughter outside first and foremost.

He went to do just that. Not thinking. Only thinking.

Only thinking of bringing his daughter out of the burning house.

Not thinking of how opening the front door and letting a fresh burst of oxygen in would ruin the rest of his life.

He opened the door, had barely allowed himself to feel relief at the fresh air, at knowing his daughter would be safe, when he felt the air rush into the house. And in that moment, he realized his mistake. But in that moment, it was too late.

He felt the fire intensify as he ran from his home, not stopping until he had placed his daughter a safe distance from the house, on the lawn near the sidewalk.

He would have run back into the house and likely died if a neighbor hadn't been there watching it all unfold. A neighbor who had tackled the desperate man. Other neighbors came and pulled him away, restrained him as he yelled and kicked and watched his house burn; his daughter hurt but safe, his son and wife unaccounted for.

Eventually, after the sirens, after the flashing lights and hoses had arrived, he felt something. Felt it while his body thrashed and he called out for his family. Felt it puncture his arm. A needle. A sedative. He slept – was knocked out – after that.

But the fire followed him even then.

And it had still been there when he had woken up in a hospital bed with his brother sitting beside him. The fire had remained as Kevin had told him that Rebecca had been able to jump out of their bedroom window when the blaze was at its harshest. He felt the fire rising in his belly as he had asked about River. When Kevin would not, could not, initially answer, that fire had overtaken Connor's heart.

He had cursed his wife for not being able to go back and get their boy, even though it had been his cigarette, his carelessness, that had started this all. That had ended it all. He blamed her. A better mother would have been able to save their boy. That's what he had said to Kevin after Kevin finally sobbed out the news about Connor's son being a boy dead of smoke inhalation, halfway cremated shortly thereafter.

Now, Connor walked along Memory Lane looking into houses here – the doors open and ablaze, the windows shattered, the curtains eaten by fire. Inside each of these houses he saw his ex-wife saving herself. Outside, he saw himself unconscious on the front lawn. As he watched this, he heard the voice of a doctor, disembodied, like it was projecting from a speaker blaring over the neighborhood. The doctor was saying,

"Unfortunately, Mr. Michaels, there was nothing that could have been done to save the life of your son..."

Saw it all, heard it all, from start to finish inside of every home on Memory Lane. And, as he watched, his grief-racked body struggling to walk along, The Pitchman's voice filled his ears. It boomed over that same loudspeaker, and from right beside him. That tinny up-tempo voice no longer sounded so soothing. No longer was reminiscent of a calming touch. As the two stood in the middle of the infinitely long road that was Memory Lane, the same identical house burning for endless miles in all directions, to Connor, The Pitchman said,

"What if you could experience it all again? What if you could relive a certain time in your life forever..."

THANKS FOR READING!

I wrote "The Fire On Memory Lane" immediately after writing my time travel novel "2222", which is part of the reason there are common elements in both stories (MEMLAIN-8/Blue Cloud Serum), though the two tales are unrelated. Both first drafts were completed in August of 2020. Both during a time when the pandemic was still fresh, and uncertainty was at an all-time high. I used nostalgia to cope with the pandemic, and I imagine many people did the same. For me it was cartoons, old movies, and way too much professional wrestling.

The conversations I had with people during the time I wrote these stories usually consisted of reminiscing about better days. What I realized then was that my conversations with others had been nostalgia-centered for a while, even before the pandemic. The older we get, the more we worship the past, obsessing over it, remembering it being better (or worse) than it was, and sometimes overdosing on it until the point we can't recover. I figured I would explore all of that in the form of a horror story.

I would love to hear your thoughts on this little trip down Memory Lane. Please leave a review on Goodreads, Amazon and anywhere else people read your opinions. It would be greatly appreciated.

Thank you to Courtney Swank for all your help and continued encouragement. And thank you to everyone who has read my work and supported me in any way. You motivate me constantly.

Like all of my books, this story is dedicated to my brother, Fred. I wish we had been given the time to make more memories.

- Dimaro
(July 11, 2021)

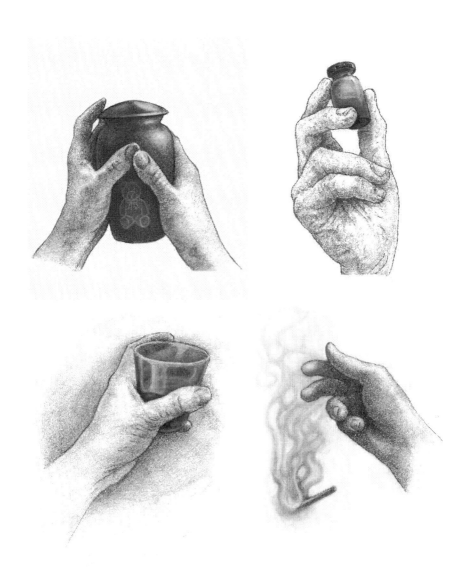

Sometimes letting go is the only option. Even when the thing you're letting go of is the fact that, once upon a time, you didn't hold on when you should have.

The Pitchman Will Return

HERE'S A PREVIEW OF

THE CORRUPTION OF PHILIP TOLES

By Felix I.D. Dimaro

COMING FALL 2021

PART ONE

STUDENT BODY

One bad October morning resulted in the ruin of so many lives.

At eight fifteen AM, on October seventeenth, before first period gym class was to begin at Rosenthal Straily Elementary School, Philip Alexander Toles – an eighth-grade student who should have been celebrating his thirteenth birthday – was found dead. Hanging by the neck from a rope attached to one of the many basketball hoops in the school's gymnasium, a painter's ladder kicked over and felled on the floor beneath him.

Gym class, of course, was cancelled that morning. As was the rest of the school day. Despondent students lingered around the school grounds, thankful for the day off from classes but not sure what to make of what had happened to their classmate. Some made fun of the suicide, hearing from their parents that those who committed the act were damned, not to be mourned. Others huddled in groups, suddenly and jarringly reminded of mortality that, to youth of that age, seems like a thing one might never have to be concerned with. Some tried desperately to understand how someone so young and so well-liked could come to the decision of suicide, while others understood the decision completely. These latter children, even amidst the mourning (or perhaps encouraged by it) thought of committing the act themselves.

After most of those confused and concerned students had cleared the grounds, teachers, equally as despondent as those students, gathered in their lounge. An impromptu staff meeting was held to discuss how things would be handled, to figure out how to move forward.

The gym teacher who had discovered the boy's body before her first period class was sitting quietly, one of many who hadn't the words to voice. Not the right words at least. Not in this situation that made no sense to her. To anyone around her.

One of the reasons so many of the teachers were silent was the result of one teacher's noise. One teacher who went from questioning "Why?" repeatedly and in a variety of ways, to crying, nearly wailing, mourning the boy as though he were her son. Several focused on consoling her. Those people were thankful for the distraction, for this vacuum of grief to allow them something to concentrate on. Something to heal and nurture. Others, however, looked at Mrs. Kathleen Jeffreys, the seventh and eighth grade Social Studies teacher, with a skeptical eye. Hers seemed to be an extreme reaction even for this situation.

Just past eleven AM, in the teacher's lounge, while Mrs. Jeffreys wailed and was comforted and was looked upon with skepticism, there was a knock on the door.

The door was answered. No one was too surprised to see the police there, politely asking to enter. Officers had been there all morning, and the teachers understood the interruption. A death had occurred, information had to be gathered, reports had to be filed. But that was not why these officers were here. They had not arrived to obtain information, but to provide it. They had several things to say to one specific person.

This already disturbing day became even more bewildering when the police asked for Mrs. Kathleen Jeffreys in particular. Everyone looked to the woman, who now not only looked bereaved but also afraid. With the presence of law enforcement in the room, some started to believe she even looked guilty. The police certainly seemed to think so as they carefully brought the woman to her feet, put her in handcuffs, and let her know just why she was being placed inside those shackles.

They spoke to Kathleen, though their words would forever be remembered by all inside the lounge. Words that would change their lives, the school, the community, many futures.

"Kathleen Jeffreys. You're under arrest for..." The officer had to pause to compose himself. Began reading from a piece of paper. A list. Each item he named adding to the horror of the day. The words he read were:

Sexual interference.

Sexual exploitation.

Sexual involvement.

Aggravated sexual assault of a child.

Unlawful sex with a minor.

Continuous sexual abuse of a child.

Conspiracy to commit kidnapping.

Online corruption of a minor.

Kathleen Jeffreys was hauled away still wailing and mourning, accused of being responsible for the corruption of Philip Toles. And his death resulting from it.

Manufactured by Amazon.ca
Bolton, ON